I0570650

CAT AND MOUSE

GENELLA DEGREY

Cat and Mouse
ISBN # 978-1-78184-728-2
©Copyright Genella DeGrey 2013
Cover Art by Posh Gosh ©Copyright December 2013
Interior text design by Claire Siemaszkiewicz
Totally Bound Publishing

Published in 2014 by Totally Bound Publishing, Newland House, The Point, Weaver Road, Lincoln, LN6 3QN, United Kingdom.

CAT AND MOUSE

Dedication

To Helena and Tim
In gratitude for your inspiration and fathomless
talents — may you be blessed with abundance, always.

A special thanks to Mark T. for the invaluable
tutelage.

Author's Note

In desperate times when our own mortality is placed
into our hands, it matters not what society thinks or
says. One does what one must to remain alive. There
is something within each of us called the survival
instinct. We are born with it and it will kick in when
the similar fight or flight instinct is drawn from the
depths of our souls.

Many of my heroines have been called, 'too modern'
for the time periods in which I write. Taking into
consideration the human survival instinct, and the fact
that my stories are fictional, the actions of my players
have never faltered from their fictive human
archetypes and the sticky situations in which they find
themselves.

I will continue to write relatable, strong heroines as I know my discerning readers will be amused by them and come back again and again for more.

Glossary of Lower-class Victorian Slang

—Source: tlucretius.net

Fine wirer — a highly skilled pickpocket
Firkytoodling — 17th century term meaning 'fondling'; Victorian slang for f**king.
Luggers — earrings
Penny gaff — low or vulgar theatre
Roger — (v) 1 the act of sex, 2 to f**k. Rogered, Rogering, etc.
Scurf — an exploitive employer or gang leader
Snatch — (n) a pickpocket or (v) stealing in a crowd
Take down — to steal
Ticker — a watch

Chapter One

The London Season, 1898

Does she have to be so bloody loud? The woman mewled like a cat in heat. *For God's sake, it's only a* rogering.

From underneath the partially refurbished rig in a fashionable London town house's repair shed, Katrina waited, ice pick in hand, for the perfect opportunity. Thankfully, the woman, who may or may not have been in the throes of passion, was too occupied with her ear-piercing song to notice when her overly-gauche diamond necklace, heavy with its glittering jewels, slid round to dangle from the back of her neck. The woman must have been hanging halfway out of the buggy door, for the top of her blonde head nearly swept the ground. Had the lamed rig wheels been attached, her coif wouldn't be in danger of attracting bits of hay and dirt from the floor—then again, Katrina wouldn't have been so well hidden in the moonlight-dappled buggy port.

It was now or never. Eyeing the stone she'd chosen to detach from the ensemble, Katrina adjusted the instrument of liberation in her grip.

The woman who'd been vocalizing her crisis, feigned or not, quieted.

"Come, Mrs Fowler, this is no time for your silence," the man doing the firkytoodling, and the front row center recipient of her concert, hissed in a strangled whisper.

"Shut up, you lout. I'm almost there," she retorted.

At once the padded bench squeaked with the vigor of a thief fleeing a crime scene. Katrina reached out to grasp the winking stone between her fingers when all at once, the entire necklace fell to the floor.

"Stop! I've lost my necklace!"

Katrina shrank to the opposite side, deeper into the shadows, her breath trapped inside her petrified lungs, and watched as the woman scrambled out of the cab to retrieve her bauble.

The wayward wife snatched it from the dirty ground and huffed out an exasperated-sounding breath. "I've had enough sport for one evening, sir."

After a few feeble protestations from the man, Mrs Fowler's pink slippers hit the dirt floor with a soft smack. She stepped a dusty, silk-clad foot into each of them and hastened from the repair shed.

Katrina's angst about being caught quickly transformed to anger. However, she found it unnecessary to verbalize her internal monologue. Readying to dismount from his makeshift love nest, the man let loose a string of scalding swearwords worthy of a sailor writing his memoirs.

She hated this—hated stealing—hated her life. And it was all her father's fault. *Damn his dead drunken soul to the Devil!*

* * * *

"I almost had it—it dangled not a pinch away from my fingertips. Had the woman's paramour been more efficient, I would have the entire necklace for you." Katrina flopped onto the nearest love seat in the dingy warehouse turned multi-nook lair. The scent of dust, likely belched up from the old seat, permeated her nostrils, causing her to hold her breath for a scant second or two.

Mr Brenner sat upon the lumpy, moldering cushion next to her. If any of the thieves who ranked above Katrina in the self-imposed hierarchy of the Den knew she could get an audience with Mr Brenner any time she chose, she'd likely be pulled into a dark alley one night and experience a thrashing for doing so. One didn't presume to be familiar with their superiors, even in the underbelly of society.

"You know, love, no one ever said life is a late-afternoon stroll through Hyde Park."

Katrina nodded and scratched her nose on the back of her fingerless black glove as he snaked his arm round her shoulders.

"And regrettably, there is no prize, nor quarter given, for a botched mission." He pulled her close so that her shoulder acted like a wedge beneath his pungent underarm. *Thank heavens for the barrier of his thick coat.* She'd smelled that pit of spoiled soup up close the very night he'd taken her under his wing—and taken her virginity as payment for the tiny space he'd let to her and the one trunk of gowns she'd refused to part with. He'd convinced her it wasn't whoring herself out, merely forging a contract between two friends.

However, Mr Brenner was *not* her friend. No, he was more like an accidental acquaintance. In her wildest dreams, she'd never have pictured herself in the same room with the sort of man who was even now attaching himself to her side like a leech.

"But I was so close!" The tears that threatened to form sounded in her voice.

"Do you know what tonight is?"

The abrupt change of subject knocked her off topic so fast it took her logic by surprise. "What?"

"Tonight marks the second month with us here at the well-oiled machine that is the East Side Den of Thieves. And you know what that means?"

She attempted to pull away discreetly. "But I tried — I've *been* trying to pick pockets and lift trinkets from the more fortunate of London — "

"I understand, I truly do. However, you agreed, of your own free will, to my payment terms. Had you been able to make rent in a more fiscal way, we wouldn't have need for a *physical* reimbursement, would we?"

Panic welled in her belly. Katrina would do anything to keep Mr Brenner's greasy attentions at bay — even if she had to pilfer a ring from the hand of Queen Victoria herself. "Wait. I — I just remembered something." She disentangled herself from him, rose and walked to the doorway — the workings in her head turning with purpose as she went. That ball tonight was a public affair, which meant anyone could come and go as they pleased. "I shall return before sunrise."

"My dear, the terms are the same if it's midnight or six in the morning."

"Yes, Mr Brenner, I am quite aware." Making sure none of the other thieves were about, Katrina slipped from the room and hurried down two corridors and a short hall to her trunk. She pulled out her oldest and least favorite gown. A yellow taffeta straight front, sporting a sheer, white, organdie overlay with daisy vines embroidered in columns around the skirt and cuffs.

She sighed—her very first ball gown. Regardless of its highly old-fashioned look, it still held the bittersweet memories of her once blossoming adulthood.

Shedding her black thieving attire and fingerless gloves that once held the sorrowful position of her mourning garb, she then quickly slipped into the daisy skirt followed by the long-sleeved bodice, then connected the corresponding eyes to the hooks below the square neckline. She pulled on the appropriate underskirts beneath the dress, tying the drawstring tightly around her waist. In compensation for wearing the gown that was all the rage ten years ago, the fabric originally taken from the last of her mother's possessions, she donned her best ivory crocheted gloves with the seed pearl trim. She recalled the time a drop of punch splashed onto her thumb. It had nearly broke her heart, but luckily, it hadn't left a stain.

Her current situation was a stain that could probably never be washed off. With much effort, she rose above the thought and focused on her mission. Her survival depended upon it.

* * * *

In no time she arrived back at the town house where the ball was still in a frenzy of gaiety. Katrina gave the doorman her coyest smile, knowing without a doubt that a lady would never do such. "I fear I'm awfully late." She allowed her eyelashes to flutter just enough to see him melt and open the door for her. With a tentative hand she reached out and ran a gloved finger down his forearm. One could catch more flies with honey, she'd learnt recently.

Not only did he allow her to pass without another word, but he bowed to her as if she were Princess Alix.

Katrina went directly to the ladies' retiring room and stood in front of one of the vanities. Strategically placed wall sconces and candelabras filled the feminine space with a soft golden light. The woman in the mirror before her looked quite the opposite of the debutantes, much younger than her own twenty-three years, who'd turned up at tonight's soirée in order to capture a husband. If any of her old acquaintances happened to be in attendance, they would never recognize her. She'd changed so very much in the last year or so. Her figure had gone from the very bud of womanhood to gaunt—her skin seemed to cling to her bones. She imagined the condition was left over from watching her father's health deteriorate.

For the last two months, following the auction of her family's estate, she'd dined on a deficient amount of less than meager fare at the Den. And aside from wearing not a single jewel this evening—every last one sold to settle the gambling debts that weren't covered by the sale of her late sire's possessions—her hair wasn't the crowning glory it used to be. During her first week with Mr Brenner, he'd persuaded her to sell her raven-black, waist-length locks to a wig-maker. He'd wrapped a strand of twine round the width and shorn her hair, just below the ears, with the biggest pair of rusty scissors she'd ever seen.

"This fist full of quids will feed you, here at the Den of course, for two months," he'd crowed and waved the paper pound notes under her nose.

She never had found out exactly how much he'd acquired, her tears had been too heavy and too frequent that night.

Katrina's morbid thoughts were interrupted by a woman who'd entered the room and lowered herself onto an upholstered bench.

"I fear I'm getting too old to stay up all night dancing." She shook her head and patted the back of her beribboned coif. The reflection in the mirror revealed her sparkling earbobs to Katrina.

"Nonsense." Katrina smiled and turned to the woman. "You couldn't be more than, what, thirty?"

The woman's fan snapped open and she giggled while the stiff white lace fluttered beneath her chin. *Chins.* "I'm a good *fifteen* years more than you suppose. Had you not been standing in the ladies' retiring room in a gown, I would have taken you for a flattering young buck." Katrina silently wondered if the woman was referring to her hair until she spoke again. "Honestly, I suppose we women should stick together. We're all we've got, after all."

She nodded but was well aware that her smile was nowhere near genuine. The conflict of guilt versus necessity pooled like a boulder in her soul. "I shall leave you to repose, then." She had turned to depart when the woman stopped her.

"Before you go, would you please help me? I think my stays have popped open at the back—I knew the drawstring was frayed, but I didn't take the time to replace it."

Katrina smiled—sincerely this time. Here, before her, was a pickpocket's dream. The woman was actually inviting Katrina to lay hands upon her person. With an inward grimace, she shifted her weight and took a step forward. What she was doing was quite wrong, and yet vital in support of her very existence. Determined, she focused on the job at hand. "Of course I will help you."

She bade the woman stand, making sure that no matter which way *Madame Baubles* turned, a mirror couldn't be seen. "The light is much better over here."

After maneuvering the layers of fabric over the woman's head, she found that the worn corset strings had merely come untied. Katrina retied the strings and, with much show and fuss, pulled the material back down over her bustle, skimming the woman's ears just enough to render them temporarily desensitised. The moment she had hold of the diamond earrings, she concealed them between her palm and thumb, then folded her hands demurely in front of her.

"Oh, thank you, my dear. It feels quite like I'm in for the duration, now."

"I consider it an honor to have helped you out."

With a nod, the woman swept from the room.

It was as if a massive weight lifted from Katrina's shoulders. She wasn't in the mood to return to the Den—now that she'd procured the required fiscal payment for Mr Brenner. She decided to wander around the upper floors of the grand town house for a while. Who knew? Perhaps she'd come across a few items that would hold her landlord at bay for at least another month if not two.

* * * *

It was near sunrise. Everyone had finally left Maxwell Courtland's Third Annual Spring Ball for their prospective homes — if not for rendezvous with their lovers. *The ton could be categorized as the biggest bunch of contradictions in history, save the Romans,* he mused as he shed his coat.

Max decided to have a nightcap in his study before heading to bed. A cap to top off the half-dozen or so other caps he'd had throughout the night. The mouth of the brandy decanter clinked cheerfully on the lip of his crystal snifter, sounding like a greeting between old friends. He lifted the beverage in a salute to no one in particular and precipitously dispensed half the glass down his throat.

The two finalists on his sister's 'Find a Wife for Max' list, had attended this evening's soirée. Weary, he lowered himself into the closest chair, feeling like a small nocturnal canine who'd narrowly escaped his captors in a summertime fox hunt.

One of the young ladies, a Miss Winifred Boonsbury, came from a very old family, but it was whispered that she was icy-cold to the touch, and, Max imagined, those doing the whispering were merely being diplomatic. With him, she neither practiced nor likely held in high regard any sort of conversational skills. The sour look cemented permanently on her face attested to the fact. And the woman's mother was so hard of hearing that the most discreet verbal exchange floated happily across any room as if she'd taken up a trumpet. If he married this girl, he'd be doomed to a silent — save the mother-in-law — wintry sort of life, which was ideal for a Christmas landscape, but Max wanted more. He wanted adventure. He wanted chemistry, heat. And, specifically, he wanted someone who'd be experimental — in bed and out.

Genella DeGrey

His other choice, a Miss Charity Wilson, was a beauty. Sadly, she'd made the rounds—flat on her back—with nearly every randy buck of the *ton*, who in turn shared the not-so-engaging experience with anyone who would listen. Apparently, she demanded expensive baubles for her *position* in society. This was not what he envisioned for his future, either. He didn't wish to spend his millions paying for the privilege of bedding *Mrs* Maxwell Courtland.

With a flip of his wrist, the rest of the brandy blazed a trail down this throat just as smoothly as the first half. The other listed females 'ripe for the picking', as his sister put it, he'd disregarded—their conditions were even worse than that of Boonsbury and Wilson. He shook his head and untied his cravat, flinging the silken tie in disgust to land where it would.

Taking up the decanter once again, he then splashed more liquid aid into his glass, the happy sound at odds with his unpleasant thoughts. He sank deeper into the chair in the darkened room and tossed back a healthy swig. Exhaling the heat from his throat, a sound startled him. It had come from behind the drapes.

"Who's there?" he demanded, rising from the chair. He set his drink down on the fireplace mantle and took up the iron and brass poker from its stand. Softly he stepped over to the window, raised the poker high above his head, grabbed hold of the thick fabric and tossed the curtain aside.

He could barely make out the figure of the little mouse of a girl who stood there. Upon closer inspection, he could discern the surprised, wide-eyed look and form of an 'O' her luscious lips held. His cock seemed to react in adolescent glee before his mind registered any further information.

Knowing he'd probably frightened her, he flung the poker to the ground. "I do apologize. I thought everyone had departed."

"I — I —"

Max motioned with his hand. "Come out. I won't harm you." He stepped out of her path so that she could pass when the sound of something large and metal hit the floor in the vicinity of her feet.

Chapter Two

"What was that?" the man asked. Amused suspicion rang in his voice. Had his face not been cast in shadow, Katrina would have been able to read which conflicting emotion prevailed. How could she tell him that the silver tray from the stunning tea service in the upstairs sitting room had just fallen from between her knees?

Katrina stepped over the tray, intending to make a dash for the door, when a hand encircled her upper arm like an iron band. A metal tinkling, albeit muffled, sounded from beneath her skirts. She drew her bottom lip between her teeth to stop herself from cursing—a habit she'd picked up from the rabble with whom she shared lodgings.

"Just a moment." He maneuvered her off her intended path and paused. "What do we have here?"

Shite! It seemed he had indeed noticed the tray on the floor.

"Hm. A thief, eh? Any other curious intrigues beneath your skirts?"

"Nothing else—I mean, this is all some sort of mistake. Unhand—"

"I think not. This situation calls for further investigation."

She tried futilely to pull free from his grip. "No... Release me this instant... Bastard!"

A strangled breath that sounded as if it could have been a humorous noise caught in his throat. "Such language, madam," he scolded.

Regardless of her struggles, he muscled her over to a settee, sat and positioned her over his knees as if she were a naughty child in need of a spanking. Bloody hell, he could have at least allowed her to face her punisher head on!

"Let me go, you cur!" She kicked her feet, but they never struck their target. This was not good. Katrina needed to escape the nightmare she'd stepped into before she ended up in Newgate.

"Stop wiggling, this instant."

At once, his hand came down on her backside. Hard. She squeaked in protest—or had she moaned?—and froze. Regardless, the sting, which refused to fade beneath the fabric of her skirts, sent liquid fire straight to her womb. She must have broken into a sweat, for the cotton of her drawers at the juncture of her thighs seemed damper than it had before. Too embarrassed to admit even to herself that the pain and pleasure of the still-smarting tap was affecting her in such a heated way, not to mention the fact that her vulnerability in this position could induce all sorts of immoral ideas, she shouted at him, "There, you've done your worst—now let me go!"

His laugh could've definitely been categorized as wicked. "That, madam, wasn't anywhere near my worst." With that, he yanked the back of her skirt up and over her bottom.

Indignant beyond words and trapped between his solid chest and rock-hard thighs, Katrina tried again to get away with more kicking and thrashing about, but the way in which he held her could not be broken. The silverware she'd fixed to her petticoat now tinkled aloud with each movement. At once she stilled. Perhaps he wouldn't notice her take. It was quite dark, after all. She drew in a breath. A warm, spicy scent invaded her senses, but only for a moment.

"What do we have here?"

Good God.

"Either you were in the midst of setting the table for supper and your skirts ingested a few essential items or in your spare time you are a wind chime."

"Release me, damn you!"

"Not until I've retrieved my family's silver."

Katrina heard each shellfish fork, butter knife and teaspoon as they were ripped from their restraints, and after enduring the inquest of her lower region in a manner only a husband had the right to do, she stiffened when he spoke. "There, that should do it." She felt him lean over and away from her to set her near-pilfered prizes upon an end table next to the settee. At that fortuitous moment, Katrina jumped from his lap. She slammed the heel of her boot down hard and with purpose on top of his foot, then ran for the door. Behind her the man roared out a name — likely that of someone in his household. The frantic, frustrated echo followed her all the way down the two-tiered set of stairs to the foyer. She pulled the heavy door open — damned if she was going to close it — and fled through the front gate, her frantic steps too loud upon the pavement for comfort.

Thank heavens she'd previously shoved the diamond earbobs so far down the front of her corset they wouldn't have become dislodged if he'd turned her upside down and shook her. Katrina dashed across the empty street from the shadows and into Hyde Park. Keeping close to bits of shrubbery and accommodating trees, she ran alongside Rotten Row as fast as her feet would fly. She daren't head straight for the Den in case someone had followed her from the location of the somewhat successful crime.

Soon Katrina came to the Rotten Row curve. After glancing around to insure safe flight, she hurried across the lane and kept to the trees, still heading west.

Finally she found herself next to Kensington Palace. How on earth she would make it back to the Den at Mews Street without raising suspicions at this time of morning—in a ball gown, no less—she had no idea. With no coin at her disposal, no connections to speak of and utterly hopeless—unless one counted the diamond earbobs hidden deep inside her corset—the uncertainty of doom lurked behind her like a shadow.

Pity the silver hadn't remained.

The vivid memory of that man's stinging reprimand came rushing back. It seemed impossible to her that the particular brand of rough handling of her posterior could induce such feelings. Katrina gritted her teeth against the sensual buzzing between her legs and crouched down in a corner at a cross-section of Kensington's outer wall. Pushing the recollection to the back of her mind, a feeling of desolation she was powerless to evade overtook her and she wept the bitter tears of despair.

All men were bastards. Her father, the king of the bastards, Mr Brenner, heir apparent, and the pond scum who'd accosted her tonight. The only male in the world who could be depended upon was Jimmy—and even that young man was prone to flirtations bordering on dangerous.

After a while she dried her cheeks with the tattered under-hem of her skirt and took a deep breath. The chilled air around her stirred as if wishing to escape the dawn. To this she could relate. Anger coupled with helplessness now replaced her fear and tied her stomach in knots. She needed to formulate a plan—a plan to get her out of this dreadful situation of theft, despondency and dissoluteness. But alas, the solution wouldn't be immediate. It could take weeks if not months—perhaps even years, God forbid. One thing that could be counted as a positive, she'd escaped tonight's botch-up and hadn't landed in Newgate.

Feeling much more at ease regarding the events of the past hour or so owing to a good cry, which always seemed to help when hopelessness overwhelmed her, she stood and dusted off her skirt. Reassuring herself that she hadn't been pursued, she headed south. Once she reached the Thames she'd follow the river east to the Den.

Not a quarter mile from Kensington Palace, the familiar clip-clop of a horse's hooves echoed off the surrounding buildings. With any luck, the rider would mind their own business, continue on and ignore her presence.

"Good morning!" a cheerful male voice hailed her from behind.

She felt her shoulders stiffen and her mind raced with phoney scenarios to the question the man would inevitably ask. Katrina smiled before turning to him as if her life had been happy and carefree since birth. "Good morning to you, too."

He slowed his horse to match her pace. "You seem to me, at first glance, a fish out of water."

Story of my life. Katrina laughed gaily as if his statement struck her as humorous and she looked up at him. "No, no. I'm just walking." His mischievous smile and green eyes were more striking than should have been legal. She peeled her gaze from his and continued on her path in silent dismissal of which she hoped he'd take the hint.

"What a fancy walking gown you have on. Has fashion finally dictated that an early morning walk must be made in formal attire?"

Wonderful. He's both thick and *nosey. And handsome, damn him.* She glanced up at him again and took note of the fact that his choice of apparel from the waist up consisted of an unkempt shirt open at the neck. She forced herself to ignore the smooth patch of skin between the starched, likely expensive cotton. "Interesting observation from someone who seems to have forgotten his waistcoat *and* his cravat."

She watched from the corner of her eye as he raised his hand to the 'V' at his chest and up to his neckline. "I... I left in a hurry. The air at dawn is so good for one's constitution, you know."

"Mmm." Katrina kept walking. This was neither the time nor the place for polite pleasantries—however ridiculous—with a man, no matter how agreeable the countenance.

"Where are you off to? Can I be of assistance?"

"No, I'm fine, thank you."

"What is your destination?"

Obviously he intended upon making this difficult. "The docks."

"The docks, you say?" he repeated incredulously.

"Mmm."

"Which docks?"

"The ones on the Thames, of course. Where else?"

"Where else, indeed."

Mercifully, a few moments of silence fell upon them and Katrina hoped he'd given up trying to engage her in conversation. Her feet hurt as did her head from walking and running hither and yon. Lack of sleep didn't bring her disposition to be anywhere near congenial, either.

"Once you reach the docks, what do you plan on doing there?"

"I—um, I'm going abroad."

"Abroad? At the beginning of the season? Think of all the parties you'll miss."

His words stung. Her new life would no longer allow her to move about with happy abandon in society, and if truth be told, she did love the season and all the balls, teas and different social gatherings. She'd been forced to forgo the last two seasons because of her father's failing health. "I s-suppose I'll just have to get along."

"From what I understand, all London ladies love to get dressed up for such pursuits."

"Sir, it's not that I don't enjoy it. I do. I just have other plans, that is all. I'll probably attend assemblies elsewhere."

"Hmm."

He sounded as if he didn't believe her. But what did she care? She was in no position to make friendships or attachments or anything that resembled what *real* people did.

"Indulge me. You say you are going abroad, to seek parties elsewhere, but with no trunks?"

Katrina wanted to scream at him to shove off, but thought better of it. "They're in the carriage, of course."

She heard the squeak of the leather saddle as he looked about. "What carriage?"

"Mine. It—it lost a wheel—back there a-ways." She motioned with a wave of her hand behind her, praying it didn't seem as ambiguous as it felt.

"Why didn't you wait with your luggage?"

"I didn't want to be late." Sadly, she couldn't figure out how to stop his relentless, annoying questions without insulting him...even though it seemed he was just *begging* her to attack his dignity.

"Late for...?"

"The journey, of course."

"So you would prefer to make your voyage without your belongings instead of wait for the next ship?"

"Sir, I'd appreciate it if you wouldn't ask me questions—"

"I'm merely—"

"Unless you'd like to tell me why you feel the need to ride about town at sunrise half dressed?"

His silence told her he wasn't disposed to discuss his affairs, sordid or not.

She almost allowed herself to think that she'd shut him up when he spoke again. "Where did you say you are from?"

"I didn't."

"No, of course not. So where are you from?"

For a moment, Katrina considered faking a coughing fit in order to either find a suitable answer or cause a diversion. Too tired to produce a physical showing, she opted to toss out the name of a town. "Cricklewood."

"Hmm," he mumbled thoughtfully. "It's a wonder you didn't take the train."

As pleasant as it was to have a conversation with someone who'd recently bathed, their repartee wasn't helping matters. At the next crossroads, she needed to turn east—*without* having to explain why. "Sir, shall we address your shirtsleeves once again or perhaps discuss your hobby of pressing a perfect stranger about their business?"

His only reaction was a choking noise, which satisfied her more than she could convey. She glanced up for a final look at him, to perhaps memorize his features, and found him staring in such an intense manner that his eyes practically reached her soul.

Tempted to fidget, she spoke instead. "I'm sure you have better things to do—and so do I. Good day then."

At the next corner she headed east without looking back.

Sadly, the sound of the horse's hooves didn't fade. She stifled a sigh.

Chapter Three

Max had to admit, she was good. The little thief could change subjects at the drop of a hat. Pity for her he'd wagered on the suspicion—and won—that she'd head straight for Hyde Park after fleeing his Hamilton Place town house. All he'd had to do was wait on the opposite side and she'd appeared like a mouse emerging from the end of a maze.

A pretty little thing, too, the way her short black hair curled around her ears and bounced against her peaches and cream cheeks as she walked. He could still recall the feel of her bottom from the swat he'd given her. Had they met under different circumstances, he'd enjoy showing her his secret playroom and presenting her posterior with a proper what for.

Before his cock pressed any harder against his fly, he forced his thoughts in a different direction. What on God's green earth had compelled her to take to thievery? Of course, one didn't walk up to someone unknown to them and inquire about their moral judgment.

"May I ask your name?"

"Why?" She narrowed her darkly-lashed, golden-brown eyes at him before turning back to the path.

"So that I might call upon you one day."

"Sir, I'm quite sure you've noticed we've not been appropriately introduced."

"Propriety for propriety's sake is one thing, but I confess, this morning has been far from normal, wouldn't you agree?"

"Considering I'm speaking to a half-dressed man, I find I'm forced to concur."

The one thing he'd been remiss about as he'd hobbled downstairs with the utmost haste in order to wake his groom not sixty minutes ago was his state of undress. He hadn't wanted her to get so far away she couldn't be caught. Much to his annoyance, once he did catch up with her, he was more interested in interrogation than an arrest. Damn his curiosity, anyway.

"Well, since you are about to go abroad, I'm sure society wouldn't frown upon us if you were to give me your name."

"Yes, they would."

Max almost smiled. "No. I'm sure of it. Besides, how would they find out?"

"Oh, you know the *ton*—their noses in everyone else's business, issuing incessant questions until either the novelty wears off or their interest is diverted elsewhere."

He felt her barbs as if she'd been throwing wadded-up sheets of paper at him—slightly bothersome yet, on the whole, ineffective. Obviously, she was educated and she knew the peculiarities of the *ton*. He was convinced now that she had originated from amongst them. Where she had picked up the curse words she'd hurled at him earlier was an altogether different matter, and one he was determined to unravel. Slowly, if needs be.

The slight breeze brought with it a hint of rotten shellfish coupled with moldering mud and human-generated pollution, indicating the nearby Thames. He realized that he didn't have much time before he was forced to let her be on her way unless he could think of something to delay her. The buildings around them seemed to close in, squeezing the street to almost alley-sized.

"You said you came from Cricklewood?"

"Yes."

"How could you possibly know so much about the crème de la crème of society all the way from the country?"

"You know how word gets around. Especially in the country."

"Mmm. Especially there."

"Oh my!"

She'd stopped to stoop down and Max brought his horse to a halt. "What is it?"

"I've a stone in my shoe."

"Here, allow me." By the time he'd swung down from his horse and made it around the beast's rump, she was gone.

"I say, young lady—where are you?" he yelled as politely as possible. There were at least five shadowed doorways through which she could have escaped. Two of them, he noticed, were terribly untidy alleyways that led... Who knew where?

Bloody hell. He dragged his hand through the top of his hair. *The little minx.*

Katrina heard him shouting after her as she ducked through yet another passageway that took her deeper into the buildings that made up the surrounding area. Despite how badly her feet hurt, she couldn't help but giggle. She was quite certain he wouldn't abandon his horse and come after her. Besides, she had pointed out to him his state of undress at least three times. Had he a sliver of decorum, which his vacillating manners told her he harbored somewhere beneath that thick mass of brown hair on the top of his head, he'd proceed straight away for home if only to don proper clothing. Upon his return she'd be long gone. Pity it was only to the Den and not abroad as she'd told him.

* * * *

It must have been an hour later when she ducked through one of the Den's secret entrances. Her very bones ached and she needed sleep like a fish needed water.

Mr Brenner seeped from a dark portal. "Ah, Katrina. I'm glad you've arrived. I waited up for you all night long."

Katrina stifled a groan. "I'm sorry you waited. I have something for you."

"Yes," he grinned like a Cheshire cat. "I was counting on it." He slid his arm around her waist.

At once she plunged her hand down her bodice and dug out the diamonds. "Here you are—my payment for this month's lodgings."

He reached out both hands to cup her offering, demonstrating his greed. "Mmm. Diamond luggers. A decent size, too. Are they real or paste?"

"Real, I assure you."

He pocketed the earbobs and gave her a bittersweet smile. "I'll let you know if I find them otherwise."

She nodded. *Yes, I'm sure you will, you blackguard.* Katrina made for her door as fast as her aching feet would take her.

Her little corner deep within the bowels of the Den remained dark regardless of the clock, but at least was substantial enough not to allow in a single draft of air. She stood just inside the portal and blinked hard in order to get used to the dimness.

"Been runnin' all night, have you, then?"

The silky Irish-accented voice had come from the direction of her cot, but she knew very well who it was. "Jimmy, you shouldn't be here."

Jimmy Lock, as he called himself, was the youngest and most productive thief Mr Brenner had at the Den. At the top of the inner hierarchy, the only person Jimmy had to answer to was Brenner himself.

Jimmy applied the burning tip of a match to a candle wick and replied. "Then where should I be?"

"Anywhere but my bed."

"Ouch. You cut me to the quick, love," he said, sounding injured, and set the candle upon her trunk next to the cot.

"I'm not your love. I'm your friend." Of course, had Jimmy *not* been seven years her junior, and had *not* been on the run from *every* bobby in Scotland Yard at *every* waking and sleeping moment, and had they met as normal people do, being his love might have appealed to her. He knew well how to flatter and fuss for such a young man, and had more than once soothed her worries away with that smooth Irish tongue of his. Figuratively speaking, that was.

"You're limping."

She detected the concern in his statement and it warmed her weary spirit. "I'll be fine."

"Had a rough night of it, did you?"

Katrina sighed. "Aside from a pair of diamond earbobs, it *was* rather hellish."

"You poor thing. Come to Jimmy." He held out his arms to her.

As tempting as the consolation he offered was, Katrina shook her head. "There is only room on that cot for one of us, and I've paid for the right to claim it as my own."

"All right, all right, I'll remove meself. But at least let me comfort and keep you company for a time."

The young man certainly knows how to tempt a woman. "Honestly, Jimmy, all I want to do is get some sleep—"

Her excuse to oust him from her hovel caught in her throat as he stood and removed a cloth from a large white bowl next to the bed. By the light of the candle, lovely steam billowed up from the clean clear water therein. Her gaze landed on the handsome young man and his smug grin.

"This is the comfort part."

"Oh, Jimmy—" She couldn't help but coo.

"Now just sit down." He guided her to the foot of the cot. "And lie back." He folded and adjusted her flat pillow so that it supported her head. The next thing she knew he had removed her shoes and peeled off her stockings.

The hot water felt like heaven on her feet. Katrina's status at the Den hadn't afforded her hot water for washing. That privilege, like everything else, had to be stolen, which she did at every opportunity—at the risk of her neck of course. Ever so gently, Jimmy submerged and massaged her sore, tired feet. She moaned when his fingers were joined by a hard, cool, slippery substance. "Is that a cake of soap?"

"Indeed it is. Lavender." With his slick fingers he gently stretched each toe backwards and forwards, then applied pressure into the arch of her foot with tiny circles.

"God, Jimmy, that's so...so..."

"What I wouldn't do to present you with a full tub o' water," he whispered and pressed his fingers into soft tendons at the tops of her feet.

"What I wouldn't do to let you."

Jimmy's fingers stilled.

Katrina pressed her lips together. The euphoria of the scent of lavender soap and the sensation of hot water lapping against her skin had almost made her lose her head. "What I meant was—"

"I know perfectly well what you meant, Katrina. Perhaps one day you will see that you and I could be great together. I'm young, virile. I can pleasure you, Katrina—like you've never been before."

Her cheeks went hot. She *hadn't* experienced pleasure before, if truth be told. Not the kind he was speaking of. Receiving said pleasure from a sexual encounter was a fairy tale. And besides, ladies didn't speak of such things. And a childish slap on the bottom from a perfect stranger didn't count, either. "Jimmy. Our circumstances could never afford—"

"We could leave this place—together. I have a decent amount stashed away—we could start over—"

"What about all that business about crossing Mr Brenner?"

"I've mentioned to the bloke that I'd like to quit the Den. Moreover, with you by my side, I wouldn't care what he and his lackeys did to me."

Katrina closed her eyes. Jimmy was a kind boy despite the fact that he was a thief and she didn't want to hurt him for the world. When she had first arrived at the Den, he'd attempted to teach her the fine art of thievery. She'd been a poor student at best.

The silence stretched on as he continued to massage her feet. Finally, Katrina opened her eyes and sat up. "It would not work between us. Could not. You must find someone your own age—and for heaven's sake, stop living this life."

He gazed at her with the sort of wisdom that his youthful blue eyes shouldn't have known. "You mean the same life you're livin'?"

On that count, he was right. It seemed her attempt to discourage his romantic advances on the grounds that their lives were too dissimilar had failed as it had numerous times before. "Jimmy, we can only be friends."

The trace of a frown crossed his features before his eyes took on that roguish sparkle once again. "*Close* friends?"

Katrina folded her arms over her chest. "*How* close?"

"*Cousin*-close." He grinned.

She couldn't help but smile back under his regard. "Oh, very well."

Jimmy raised and held her ankles above the bowl. "Your water's gone tepid." He reached over, took up the cloth he'd discarded earlier and gently dried her feet.

"Thank you. You are very sweet, you know."

"Remember that little sentiment, *cousin*." He winked at her. "Now let me help you off with your gown."

"I don't think—"

"Did I take advantage of you when your legs were naked and at my mercy?"

She sighed, resigned. "No."

"Then allow me to assist you."

She was sure that had she not been this exhausted, she wouldn't have complied so easily.

Once Jimmy had the gown in his hands, she felt as if she never wanted to see it again. It no longer reminded her of her mother, the fabric was now tainted with the memory of the worst attempt yet at her new…profession.

Katrina scoffed. "Just, just toss that anywhere. On the floor in the corner would be fine."

Soon he had her tucked, still in her underpinnings, beneath the threadbare top sheet that doubled for a coverlet.

"Now I'd stay, but I need to get to work. There are plenty of heavy pockets out there in need of light'nin'." Jimmy kissed her on the forehead and made for the door.

"Be cautious, Jimmy."

He stopped at the portal and tossed her a mischievous look. "Aw, you care after all. I'm touched."

Then he was gone.

* * * *

Max tossed his shirtsleeves into a corner and fell face down on his bed. He'd stood there on that bloody street yelling for the girl for at least five minutes. *Five minutes…* He argued with himself. *After all it doesn't really seem like a long period of time, unless one is talking to one's self. Then it can be an eternity.* "Oh for God's sake." This was not like him at all.

Indeed, the fact that she was out there, all alone, was enough to churn his insides to a creamy acidic mess…but those eyes of hers—haunting, greenish-yellow and almond-shaped. In the cat-like depths a distinct combination of mistrust and fear fought to hold court like oil and water.

Genella DeGrey

She was hiding something...many somethings.

Furthermore, he didn't believe for a second that his little mouse intended to travel to the continent. No woman, not even one of slim means, would venture forth without her trunks, or at the very least, a valise—not to mention an escort. It was now obvious to him as day. She'd been lying. There was no journey in her future.

The beginning of the season was upon them—no doubt she'd turn up at one of the other balls around town to commit her thievery. He'd just have to keep one eye open for her at all times.

"There you are, sir. I wondered where you'd gotten off to." Walters, Max's personal valet and trusted confidant, threw open the curtains at the far end of the room.

Max turned his head to speak. "If you don't mind, Walters, I'd like to sleep until supper."

"Long night?" Walters asked and redrew the heavy wine-colored velvet brocade fabric.

"Day, night, morning. All of it tedious." Then a vision of the little mouse flitted through his mind. "Well, most of it."

Walters strode over to the bed and replaced the nub of a candle with a new one from a drawer. "Tea, sausage, eggs and potatoes are on the way up. Shall I tell Simmons—?"

"No, that will be fine. I'll eat and sleep afterwards. Please hold all correspondence until I'm myself again. And *no* callers."

"Not even Miss Susanna?"

"Don't you mean Lady Kendrick, wife of Lord Charles Kendrick?" He rolled over and eyed the elder valet who'd been with Max all of his adult life.

"My mistake, sir. No matter how long your sister has been or ever will be married, I will always think of her as Miss Susanna."

"Yes, well, don't be surprised if her husband takes personal offense." Max observed a slight twitch in Walters' lips.

"I shan't, sir."

At that moment, Simmons the butler knocked then brought in Max's breakfast—*The Morning Post* tucked neatly to one side of the tray as always. Walters helped set Max up with the meal. As his staff made to take their leave, he reiterated, "Remember, no visitors—*Especially* Susanna."

"Yoo-hoo!" A feminine voice drifted from the hallway into his room and a sweet face peeked around the door frame, so familiar to him that he could close his eyes and see it—which was exactly what he chose to do.

"Maxwell Courtland, you lazy boy. Rise and shine!" She sauntered into the room.

"Hello, Susanna," Max sighed and popped a sausage into his mouth.

Chapter Four

"I can't believe you are still abed on this glorious day!"

Max shrugged as his mouth was full.

"My, but it's dark in here. Did you choose between Charity or Winifred last night? I'm leaning toward you taking Charity for your wife."

He swallowed. "I chose not to choose."

Susanna flopped unladylike onto the settee beneath a south-facing window. "But why?"

God, how he hated it when she whined. "Not ready." He took a bite of his potatoes.

Her gaze swept across the ceiling as she spoke. "Not ready—what a silly thing to say."

"It isn't when you're truly *not ready*."

"Well, what does that mean anyway? I long to plan another wedding and you aren't helping."

"My dear Susanna," he said and wiped his mouth on a linen napkin. "You've already had a wedding. As for the wedding in question, the marriage hasn't even been arranged yet. Furthermore, the bride, who is yet to be chosen, will likely wish to plan it herself."

"Yes, but I'm sure she'll want, even *need* my advice. I'm terribly experienced in the latest, you know."

"The whole of London is overwhelmed with your amount of experience."

"Oh, don't embellish so. Why haven't you chosen a wife yet? I gave you a perfectly good list from which to make your selection."

He'd never noticed it before, but did all women have the aptitude for chatter—and on several different topics in one breath? "You did give me a list." He nodded. "As for 'perfectly good', I have my doubts."

She harrumphed. "I'll have you know that several of the dowagers about town helped me put that list together."

"I'm sure they did—and I'm also positive they added their own relations to the record at every opportunity."

Susanna opened her mouth to speak but apparently thought better of it. Her shoulders slumped and she chewed on the inside of her cheek.

Satisfied that her mouth was involved in an alternate pursuit, however temporary, he bit into another sausage. After finishing most of the eggs and potatoes, he felt contrite about being so harsh with his little sister. "Now, now, Susanna. I—I just thought that perhaps there were one or two more you may have accidentally left off that list."

This perked her up and she asked, "But who? I made sure every good family with eligible daughters—"

"Did you happen to see a young lady with short, black hair last night at my ball?" Just speaking of the little mouse made him want to give in to a ludicrous smile, which, at that very moment, tugged at the corners of his mouth. Max took up his tea cup and occupied his lips with sipping.

"Short hair?"

He swallowed. "Yes, it sort of—well, curled 'round her ears to cling close to her cheeks."

Max watched her eyebrows knit together. "How very unfashionable."

"Sometimes what's fashionable isn't always attractive," he said in the mouse's defense and set his tea down upon the tray. "So you didn't see her, then?"

"I don't think so. I would have remembered something so—so—"

"Different?"

Susanna smiled. "What a very diplomatic way of putting it, Maxwell."

He quelled another grin and dabbed the corners of his mouth with a napkin. His sister had always been caught up in the fashion of the moment, but she was even worse lately—her new husband being a relation to a member of the elite *ton*, even if he was only a barrister. Max thought he'd arranged an excellent match with the two of them, if he did say so himself. "Regardless. I didn't procure an introduction because... Well, because I wasn't sure from whom to garner it."

"You mean she went to a ball without an escort? Really, Maxwell. You should have acquired better judgment by now. Those are the types of girl one only toys with, not ones who deserve a marriage proposal."

"That's not a fair statement, Susanna. Perhaps when I noticed her, the escort was...behind a pillar."

"Oh yes, that must be it. After all, you have so very many fat pillars in your ballroom— Hey!"

Susanna shouldn't have been so surprised when his wadded-up, linen napkin bounced off her chin and into her lap.

"Hm. Perhaps you aren't ready for matrimony. You still act like a child." She tossed his napkin onto the bed.

Max chuckled. He knew he'd won a small scuffle, but was leagues away from winning the entire war.

"Oh, Maxwell," she huffed. "You're so spoiled! You always get your own way — always get everything you go after, no matter the stakes. I've a mind to place an advertisement in *The Primrose League Gazette* and have the women line up at your door as if you were interviewing housekeepers. That would show you."

"Look, *Stinker.*" He used the nickname she'd hated as a child and despised as an adolescent. "There's no need for all that. Just do me the small favor of holding back the invitations to my wedding until I've — "

"Explored every crowded avenue and dubious alleyway?"

" — chosen a bride, all right?"

His sister pouted prettily and shrugged a shoulder — which meant she agreed.

Susanna declined his offer to order up breakfast for her and announced she had other morning calls to make. She kissed him on the cheek and bade him farewell.

Once Susanna had departed, Max set aside his tray, reclined onto the stack of pillows at his back and proceeded to construe the whos, whats and wheres about his wonderful new obsession — for which he refused to chastise himself. Everyone needed something to occupy themselves, after all. He grinned inwardly and set his mind to the task before him.

The more he dwelt upon them, the visual facts from this morning stated the evidence loud and clear. He ticked off the evidence in his mind. There was no way in hell the mouse was for the continent — not in a ball gown more suited for a girl just out, and without any feminine equipage whatsoever. It was apparent she hadn't of late circulated in high society. She had a certain savvy about the streets one only achieved by living so roughly for an extended period of time. However, her refined manners—not counting her insalubrious vocabulary—told another story.

With this realization, his heart broke for the girl who had been obviously forced into a dishonorable lifestyle. Likely she'd had a man in her life and the coward had betrayed her, causing her to have to turn to pilfering. Once he found her, and earned her trust, he'd get his hands on the blighter who'd done this to her. Heaven help the poor man when he did.

But first to find her.

Of course, this meant he'd not only have to keep his eyes open when on the streets and his ears open to any gossip that sounded remotely recognizable, but he'd also have to make an appearance at every public ball this season. At such events one usually encountered the same faces, so if his hunch was correct, the mouse would be there—as would the chilly Miss Winifred Boonsbury and wretched Miss Charity Wilson.

However, if all this fuss led to finding his mouse, it would be worth it. Max sighed—half in resignation, half at the very thought of being in her presence. He reached for *The Post* and flipped through to the society page to chart out the parties he'd need to attend in order to set his trap.

* * * *

Katrina stretched her arms above her head, unaware as to what time of day it was. She'd slept rather soundly and felt far bloody better than she had when she'd retired the night, or rather morning before.

She arose from her cot, donned her plain mourning gown and made her way to where the Den's food supply lay. They'd set up an old wood burning stove and had procured several pots and pans with which to cook. Everyone pitched in to make sure there was water and fuel available for kitchen purposes. In addition, each person was required to clean up after themselves. More than once Katrina had wished the former rule could be applied to the world beyond. London, for one, wouldn't be such a miserable, filthy place if people weren't so untidy with their personal flotsam and jetsam.

By the way the shadows fell high upon the wall beneath the small, open window near the ceiling, it must have been late afternoon. She plucked a jar of apple preserves from a shelf, but how she would serve it eluded her.

If only one of those silver spoons would have made it back to the Den with me last night. Katrina recalled with a bitter taste on her tongue and a maddening irritation at just how she'd been divested of the items. *Damnation.* That man could have done all sorts of damage to her person—let alone her situation. He could have kept her there until the authorities arrived. The very thought of life in Newgate made her stomach roil. She took a deep breath to shake off the sinking feeling in her gut.

She then recalled the second man, the one who'd followed her and almost foiled her plans of returning to the Den without being noticed. Who was he and what had possessed him to tag along and put so many questions to her? He was indeed a handsome gent—

even in his disheveled state of undress. It wasn't that he couldn't attract any woman he set his sights for —

"You bring the fruit and I'll provide a bit o' bread."

Katrina glanced up to see Jimmy standing in the doorway with a loaf of bread tucked smartly under his arm.

She made to comment when, from behind him, Mr Brenner appeared and clapped him soundly upon the back. "We celebrate *together*. I brought the ale." He pushed past Jimmy and plunked down a small crate of four bottles. The jolt made the rickety wooden table rock upon its three good legs. The few ramshackle chairs were just as healthy looking. But who was she to complain? She hadn't a stick of furniture to her name.

Jimmy's smile didn't come near to engaging the rest of his features and his disposition shifted with an odd sort of tension about his neck and shoulders. Something was out of joint. Mr Brenner's praise only brought forth a hard coldness from Jimmy that Katrina had never seen before. Under normal circumstances, Jimmy exuded conviviality.

"And what exactly are we celebrating, gentlemen?" Katrina asked as she eyed the two men.

"Mr Lock has just found his self in the winners' circle — broken his own record, as far as fine wirers go."

"Indeed?" Katrina commented and gingerly placed the preserves upon the table.

Mr Brenner held up a hand, knuckles facing her with his thumb tucked into his palm. "He took down no less than *four* gold tickers in the same amount of time."

Katrina hid a wince and ran her fingers through her hair. Stealing was wrong — even though she did it to survive. It was a conundrum she'd lived with every day since she'd begun at the Den. If a child was starving was it wrong to steal a bite of food for him? She'd gone round and round in her head with questions of the like. Once again she pushed the conscience-scouring to the back of her mind. It was one thing to reproach one's self, but she wasn't in the position to admonish someone else about their morals.

"Quite impressive, Mr Lock." She nodded even though it felt like she'd been socked in the stomach without her woman's under-trappings for protection.

Mr Brenner pulled out a chair for her and she sat. "I'm still convinced you could do even better. Perhaps a bit more tutelage under Mr Lock would do it."

Jimmy lifted his eyebrows briefly and swung his leg over the back of his chair. He sat and reached for a bottle of ale. He flipped the wire to release the stopper, took a long draw and his countenance changed once again to congenial. "Having Miss Katrina under me again would be my greatest pleasure."

Katrina tucked his mood swing to the back of her mind for further inspection and shook her head. "I'm sure what you have in mind is not exactly what Mr Brenner meant." She tore off hunks of bread and distributed them.

"Perhaps not, love—" Jimmy winked at her. "But if it were, I could charge admission and make out rather well."

Mr Brenner burst forth with an exploding guffaw. "Yes, *we* could. Like having me own penny gaff. I like the way you think, Mr Lock."

"Sorry, chaps." Katrina was determined to speak to them on their own level in order to quell this horrifying idea. "I've no mind to star in your bloody peep show, so forget it was ever mentioned."

Jimmy shrugged. "Well, anyways, I agree. You and me ought to do some jobs together. It's an enterprizin' idea at least."

"Good boy," Mr Brenner said in a peculiar, warning-like tone. "'Tis the season, after all, when the gentry of society open their doors to the public for parties and such." Mr Brenner popped open his ale. "Perhaps Miss Katrina can snatch up another pair of sparkly baubles like she did last night."

Jimmy turned to Katrina. "Are we for it, then?"

She shook her head. "I don't think so. It's too soon for me to go back into the crush."

"Nonsense." Mr Brenner waved a hand. "We'll fix it so you won't be recognized."

"Let me guess, gentlemen. A masked ball?"

Mr Brenner chuckled. "As beneficial as you donning a mask would be to our cause, no. I've found that the nosiest gossips are especially active during those times—owing to all the bed hopping." He glanced at Jimmy and waggled his eyebrows.

Brenner turned to Katrina. "This evening we'll fix up your hair and you can wear one of your other gowns. You have them along for a reason, don't you? They need to earn their keep as well as anything, I'd imagine."

She clenched her fists and felt her nails dig into the palms of her hands as they rested in her lap. It seemed she wouldn't be able to squirm out of this one if she fell over with a fever. "Well, I'll have to be overly cautious. Don't expect me to produce more diamonds at the drop of a hat, Mr Brenner."

He grinned at her. "Produce, no. Procure, yes."

Jimmy drew a knife from beneath his wrist cuff and spread the fruit first onto Katrina's bread then his own. "I look forward to our little outing, Miss Katrina."

Katrina wanted to sink into the floor and disappear. She'd told that man this morning she was on her way to the continent. If he happened to be in attendance tonight—and he seemed the type to be such—she was done for.

Chapter Five

"Lady Frost." Max bowed over his hostess hand. "Always a pleasure."

"Why if it isn't Mr Maxwell Courtland." Her parchment cheeks took on a ruddy flush. "I'm deeply honored you've come tonight. You'll add elegance to our décor for certain."

"Me, madam?" He released her fingers. "It is my understanding that your gatherings have always topped the season in ornamentation."

"Oh, go on," she said and waved a hand in the air. "Save your flattery for the younger set of females who've come tonight for just such attentions."

Max winked at her and continued through the entrance hall, following the strains of stringed music to the ball room. The dance card, which had been pressed into his palm by the coat room attendant, dangled from his wrist. With any luck he'd have his little mouse's name before the night was over — provided she made an appearance. He admitted it would be a daring move on her part if she were to show her face, but if she was anything, she was bold.

He glanced around the ballroom. "Come out, come out, where ever you are," he breathed his challenge. Max nearly chuckled aloud. He didn't even know her name and she'd occupied his thoughts since their first encounter in his study.

Somehow, and quite annoyingly, his imagination dug up Susanna's convictions. Would the mouse have a chaperone with her this time? Did common rabble — or *un*common in her case — have access to chaperones? He couldn't imagine her wearing that same gown. Women, no matter their station, didn't do such things for formal events — or so Susanna had told him on occasion.

One thing Max was certain of, he'd recognize her by her hair. The raven-black, curved at the ends, hand-length tresses... He could see himself sitting behind her in a tub of hot water, his fingers knuckle-deep with suds as he shampooed her hair. God, what a vision she would be — her pale skin soaking up fragrant French bath oils — and what he would do to her body afterwards...

He took a steadying breath. *Damnation.* How long would he have to fantasize about her before she was in his arms?

For now, he'd have to bide his time. Hoping to cool his thoughts, he chose to do a goodly amount of this at the punch bowl, before he went about with an embarrassing cockstand.

Katrina stood in a crush of people and glanced up at the impressive three-story edifice in which tonight's public ball would be held. She felt Jimmy, who had her gloved fingers tucked securely into the crook of his elbow, twitch once in a while. Likely, he was snatching items from the crowd around them. Mr

Brenner had high hopes for the evening's take, and with Jimmy along, it promised not to disappoint.

Back at the Den she'd dressed in her cream satin ball gown, which could have used a good taking in at the chest. It was vastly more fashionable than any of her other gowns, though, with its large puffy sleeves and no bustle. Jimmy had brought hairpins with paste diamonds affixed to the tips—courtesy of Mr Brenner's 'un-sellable stash'. He'd helped her to twist her hair up and secure the loose rolls with the pins. She had to admit she didn't look nearly as obvious tonight as she had last night.

"Pity we're working." He leaned toward her and whispered, "I could have used a night of leisure with you on my arm."

"Young ladies don't attend events with gentlemen alone. *Chaperones* accompany them," she informed him in a lowered voice.

"Damn—I'm fresh out o' chaperones."

She turned to him. "And no matter how good you are, I'm quite certain you couldn't pluck one of those from the crowd."

"Now there ya got me. My pockets are too small to accommodate such haulage."

His quip made her grin. Regardless of his dashing good looks and how handsome he appeared in his very fashionable evening attire, Katrina imagined his Irish lilt would give him away were he to speak to anyone. "Jimmy, about your…accent."

"Don't you worry yourself, love. I know when to sound like an English blue-blood."

"This promises to be interesting," she teased and he tossed her a 'just watch me' look.

They approached the door and Katrina felt nervous for the first time that evening. It wasn't the fact that she and Jimmy attended together to pilfer goods for Mr Brenner, although that did poise her nerves on the brink somewhat, but her anxiety rose when she thought of that tall, green-eyed man whom she'd eluded that morning. Would he be there tonight? All at once the bloody, niggling thought wouldn't let her be. If he did turn up and recognize her, she'd have to come up with an excuse as to why she had stayed in London and not taken her journey. *And he would ask, too. The meddlesome twit. Handsome, meddlesome twit,* she amended.

Katrina quietly scolded herself for the direction of her thoughts. Determined to succeed tonight, no matter the circumstance, she handed her caplet to the coat room attendant and accepted her dance card. Glancing down, she realized that she hadn't seen one of those in what seemed like ages. She recalled them fondly from her coming-out. The silken cord with the tiny pencil attached, the names of the dancers scrawled across the lines — each in distinctive bold handwriting. With gloved fingers she caressed the card and a pair of laughing green eyes penetrated her subconscious. Pity she couldn't fill it with the name of a certain inquisitive, broad-shouldered... *No!* She stopped herself before the thought could come to fruition. Tonight she was here to do a job. She swallowed against the tide of emotions and she and Jimmy slipped into the crowd surrounding the dance floor.

Jimmy told her he considered it a boon that, because of the Grand March, each and every one of his victims paraded by him. It presented a chance to pick and choose whose pockets and purses to pluck at throughout the evening.

Katrina took up a position behind a tall fern in case Mi'lord Curious from this morning happened by. Luckily, he didn't seem to be amongst the revelers, but the fashionables had always considered being late *the thing*. Had she the means, she'd set her own invitation time two hours before her ball actually started. That would show them.

"Bloody rich throng, don't you think?"

Pulled from her wandering reflections, Katrina turned toward Jimmy. "I beg your pardon?"

"The baubles and such—like taking sweets from a baby. No, it's like taking sweets from a baby who's offering me what's in her hand."

She jerked her chin in the opposite direction and hoped he didn't take offense. Although it didn't have to do with Jimmy personally, it did sicken her so to dwell upon the thievery part of the evening.

"I thought I might find you here near the refreshments."

Max's eyes burned from scanning the crowd. "Whatever do you mean, Lady Kendrick?"

"Hiding. Hiding from your future obligations. And don't call me Lady Kendrick. It sounds as if you are speaking to my mother-in-law, for heaven's sake."

"All right, *Stinker*."

"Ooooh, Maxwell, you are insufferable."

"What are big brothers for?" Leading her further away from the subject at hand, he tuned to focus his attention on her. "And where is his lordship tonight?"

"Taking brandy in one of the parlors. He's just about to make his intentions fully public."

"Which intentions are those?"

"Why, his aspirations to elevate to judge. Haven't you heard a word I've said about it for the past fortnight?"

"I have. And I still think it odd that he decided to earn a living as a barrister instead of enjoying his fortune like his father."

"My Charles is a modern sort of fellow with a brilliant mind. You should be thankful he wants more for me and our family than just his family's scraps."

Max grunted. He couldn't argue with that. "But isn't he a bit young for a judge?"

"That's just the point, silly. He'll be the youngest judge in history—*if* the Lord Chancellor finds him worthy, that is. And after he publishes his article for *The Morning Post* on the benefits of having opposing attorneys in the court room, he's sure to get silk in no time. In fact, I have a rough draft of his article right here in my reticule." She patted the velvet pouch that hung from the crook of her elbow by a delicate chain. "It's quite brilliant, really, considering the justice system, up until recently, only had the prosecuting attorney in attendance."

"And where do you fit in this scheme?"

"It's not a *scheme*. Charles is having me keep it safe."

"What will you do with your husband's pages, stitch a bit of lace on each one?"

She stared at him with a straight face and a dull look in her eye. "You know, you are so clever, Maxwell. Your humor is simply awe-inspiring." He was just about to ask if she'd seen the elusive, short-haired girl when she spoke again. "For your information, Charles trusts me above anyone of our acquaintance."

Charles' plan was solid, Max had to admit, but there were other matters occupying his mind tonight. "Well, all the best. Now I really need to get back to…"

Susanna tilted her head when he paused, likely expecting him to continue. Which he didn't. "Get back to…?"

"Surveying…for pick-pockets…on behalf of Lady Frost. This being a public affair and all. She is concerned, you see." He couldn't stand fibbing to his sister, but more than a few precious moments—which could be better spent watching for his mouse in the crowd—were slipping through his fingers.

"So watching for thieves is how you will be spending your evening? I believe that's the worst thing I've ever heard." She huffed out a breath. "At least try to dance, especially if your two list-toppers make an appearance tonight."

If by list-toppers she meant the mouse, he'd gladly do so. "I promise."

She eyed him up and down. "For some odd, niggling reason—perhaps it is because you so readily agreed—I don't believe you."

"Susanna—"

"I've a mind to tell Charles to go on home without me and have you escort me there later."

"So that you can dance more freely with the gentlemen at this gala?" His intention of throwing her off the scent missed by at least a league.

"No, so that I can make sure *you* do your duty and dance with Miss Boonsbury and Miss Wilson."

Max coughed out a harrumph.

"If Charles agrees, I shall return to motivate you. And you'd best not disappoint me, brother."

"I need a reprieve. Come dance with me, Miss Katrina," Jimmy murmured from behind her. Soft hairs that had fallen from her coiffeur onto her neck stirred at his breathed words and sent a wave of relaxation over her skin.

"I shouldn't."

"Indeed you should. It's me, Jimmy, remember? And you must indulge your *cousin* at least once out of sheer politeness."

Katrina hid her grin behind a sigh. She slipped her dance card from her wrist and handed it to him. He in turn released his to her.

"The last waltz in the set, I think."

"You know how to waltz, Jimmy?"

"Me ma was a dancer — of sorts," he said and scrawled his name across from the appropriate dance. "You'd be surprised at the things I know."

She doubted she'd be shocked at his disclosure and it likely shone in her eyes.

"Come now. I haven't been a pilfering scamp all my life."

Katrina signed her first name upon the line and each returned their card to the other.

"Oh, and before I forget, I'll need you to hold this for me." He dug into his pocket, fished out a handful of something he kept concealed in his fist. "My trouser pockets are threadbare and I'm certain the weight of it will cause this evening's take to escape through the fabric."

Her hand received what he offered and she quickly tossed it down the front of her gown. It was indeed weighty, but she'd carry it for her friend.

"Mm. I'll have to find more for you to cache for me." He winked. "Come on then. Our dance is after this quadrille."

Max successfully avoided Miss Boonsbury and Miss Wilson by stationing himself between the back wall and one of the many tall potted ferns in the room. The décor in the Greco-Roman style seemed a bit outdated but well done nonetheless. The semi-sheer swag draperies hung in layers from the ceiling, disguising corners as if the space stretched unremittingly like a parlor on Mount Olympus. He made to observe the style of the flooring. However, there were so many dancers about, it wasn't easy to discern the placement of the marble tiles.

A woman in a fashionable cream ball gown floated by, preoccupied with the waltz in which she was engaged. He absently admired the jewels in her dark hair and how they winked at him even in the modest candlelight.

At once a temporary shock wave shot through his body.

It was the mouse—and the young man with whom she danced was in danger of receiving a beating from Max, for he held her far too close.

Chapter Six

"I thank you, my lord." Susanna dipped an elegant curtsey to her husband after he'd granted her the rest of the evening to spend with her brother. She left the parlor and squeezed through the crush on the way to the refreshment table where she'd last seen Maxwell.

"Hello, Lady Kendrick."

"Why, Charity Wilson." Susanna paused and smiled at the girl who topped her brother's list of possible wives. "How are you this evening?"

"I'd be better if I could find your brother."

"I'm on my way to meet him now. Would you care to join me?"

"Oh, no. It is my understanding that men like to make chase, not the opposite."

"I see. Well, I'll certainly put in a good word for you, dear. In fact, I'd be surprised if you weren't engaged by season's end. "

"That would be lovely of you. M'ma says I couldn't do better than Maxwell Courtland financially." Charity made an elegant curtsey and Susanna nodded back.

Upon her arrival at the refreshment table, Susanna noticed her brother's absence immediately. "He's done this on purpose. And it's just like him to do so," she murmured, feeling as if she were back in rompers again. Her brother had been a terrible tease, hiding her favorite dolls, fibbing about her parentage, telling her scary stories until she was unable to sleep—and that awful name he'd called her. Susanna nearly shuddered at the thought of him insisting his friends call her *Stinker* as well.

Shaking off the sour memories, she scanned the room for Maxwell and tapped her toes to the tune of the waltz, albeit impatiently. There was no one within shouting distance whom she had an acquaintance with—or with whom she'd like to spend some time chatting. She lifted her elbow and reached around for her bag. If she had a few moments before Maxwell emerged, she could pull out one of her—

Susanna's breath filled her throat in a rush. Her reticule was gone.

Katrina would've been happy to confess to Jimmy the fact that he was indeed an exceptional dancer if it wouldn't have put the idea into his head that a flirtation was acceptable between them. His lead was such that he practically steered her across the floor, never once running into the other couples who whirled around them at different speeds.

It had been so long since she had had any sort of vigorous exercise—notwithstanding the walking to and from the Den. Katrina acutely felt the heat of the room and its occupants as if they pressed at her from all sides. She lifted her chin to seek out a breath of fresh air when her gaze landed on a pair of startled green eyes.

"Bloody hell," came her strangled expletive.

"What is it, love?" Jimmy asked as they whirled closer to the front of the ballroom.

"I—" She swallowed hard. "I think there is someone here who recognizes me."

"Bollocks. Let's get you out o' here." As they hurried through the crush at the edge of the dance floor, Jimmy whispered, "Meet me five blocks east and five to the south. Don't let anyone follow you." Then he melted into the crowd.

Without thinking, Katrina turned and slammed into a young woman whose eyes shimmered with tears.

"Could you please help me?" She issued her plea directly to Katrina. "I think my reticule has been stolen."

Damnation. Am I wearing a badge that signifies me as a bobby for bloody sakes? "Miss, I cannot help you. I have troubles of my own." She made to turn away when the girl took hold of her arm.

"But you *must* help me! I'll be in the gravest of trouble if you don't!"

If anyone knew what it was like to need assistance and a friendly face it was Katrina. Before another thought could blossom, she took hold of the girl's hand and yanked her through the breezeway, zigzagging around formerly attired attendants and out of the front door.

Katrina pulled her along to weave in between and around people, carriages and horse leavings.

"Where are we going?" the girl stammered from behind her.

Retrieving an answer from who knew where, Katrina replied, "Somewhere we can talk in private."

"But I last had my reticule at the Frosts' —"

Katrina ignored the girl's plea and hastened her steps, dragging the chit behind her. It was the girl's own fault. Had she not insisted that Katrina help her, she'd still be at the Frosts' ball, annoying someone else.

Just before they made the first turn heading south, Katrina slowed to take a peek behind them. A tall, brooding man, the very same one who'd found her walking this morning, was at least a block away, bounding toward them at a smart pace.

"Shite," Katrina cursed under her breath. She turned and sped up their pace.

"I — I beg your pardon?" her new partner squeaked.

"You'd better move those feet of yours if you want my help."

It was quite apparent that the girl wanted Katrina's aid, for she practically ran ahead of her.

A couple of houses before the corner where she was to meet Jimmy, she ducked into a small yard, searching for a place where she and her new hanger-on could hide. Thankfully, the residence and yard were substantial and the brick pathway continued alongside the house, deep into the shadows.

"This way." She pulled the girl along the side yard, their soft ball slippers like whispering taps upon the bricks amidst the swishing of satin skirts. They hurried past a precious set of heavy wrought-iron table and chairs painted white, which practically glowed against the darkness. Oh, to have the luxury of the occasion for a garden tea back in her life, Katrina mused briefly. They continued along the hedgerow speckled with tiny light-colored flowers and passed a fountain adorned with cherubs. After turning on the path that led behind the house she stopped, peeked around the corner whence they'd come and waited, both of them panting like a couple of racehorses.

"Be extremely quiet for a few moments." She barely got the words out when she saw the man run in and out of her view of the street.

Katrina heaved in a breath and let it out in utter relief. "Thank heavens." He hadn't seen them duck into the yard.

"What was so urgent that we had to flee?" the girl whispered to Katrina.

"I—" Katrina thought to appeal to her new friend's feminine sensibilities. "I'm avoiding an unwanted encounter with a certain gentleman."

"Oh my. From whom do you run?"

Katrina felt her cheeks heat in her embarrassment. "To be quite honest with you, I don't actually know his name."

"Ah. One of *those*. I understand completely. Had a couple in my day."

Katrina took a closer look at the girl at her side and nearly laughed. *A couple?* With her large, wide set eyes, sweet feminine voice and porcelain skin, there was no question as to why men would have found her attractive. However, she seemed extraordinarily youthful to have suffered too many situations. "You couldn't be more than, what, nineteen or twenty?"

"Twenty-one this summer, but I assure you, before my brother, Maxwell, intervened and found me a suitable match, undesirable men buzzed around me like flies." She shuddered.

"Come. Let me see if he's gone." Katrina inched her way toward the front of the residence, keeping close to the wall in case he retraced his steps. At the corner she backed the girl up against the house with an outstretched arm and peeked around, trying to keep the entirety of her body concealed.

"Unbelievable."

"What? What's wrong?"

"Stay hidden. He's...lurking."

"Oh, dear." The girl pressed herself against the wall as if she wanted to sink into the brick façade.

In actuality, her pursuer had found Jimmy as he waited for her on the corner. It looked like the stranger had engaged her partner in conversation. In order for Jimmy not to look suspicious, she was sure he was forced to accommodate the nosey bugger. Damnation, if he wasn't in the midst of interrogating Jimmy as he had her that very morning...

"How long do you think he'll choose to *lurk*?"

"There's no telling."

A few moments of silence fell between them while Katrina watched Jimmy converse with the man. Jimmy's expertly casual stance didn't fool her for a moment. He was a sly genius, but Katrina could distinguish his method of placation from all the time they'd spent together observing people's public faces and tells.

The girl tapped Katrina on the shoulder and whispered. "I know this is terribly against proper decorum, but my name is Lady Susanna Kendrick. I am the wife of Lord Charles Kendrick."

Katrina turned to the girl. "I—" the situation was getting more complicated by the moment. "You can call me Miss Katrina."

"Oh, but—" she paused for a moment then continued. "Then please call me Susanna."

She presented her newest acquaintance a nod in lieu of a curtsey and returned her attention to the corner across the street. Her pursuer was in the process of lighting a cigar, then held the flame for Jimmy.

A groan escaped from between Katrina's lips.

"What is it now?"

"I believe we've been granted some time to get acquainted." Katrina led Susanna down the path to where the garden chairs sat and together they lowered themselves to the seats. "Now, tell me. What was so important back there at the ball?"

"Oh, it's just awful. My reticule has been stolen."

"That's what all—" Katrina subdued the snide remark and cleared her throat. "How do you know you didn't just leave it somewhere accidentally? The cloakroom, for instance."

"I would never do such a thing! I had personal items therein that mean the world to me."

"We all carry items of that nature on our persons. Are you certain—?"

"Begging your pardon, Miss Katrina," she interrupted with the utmost politeness. "You see, my husband entrusted me with an article he's written—a very important article that will directly affect his—*our* future." Lady Susanna let out an exasperated sigh. "And there is more."

"Let me guess. Letters from your lover?"

Lady Susanna's eyes went wide. "Bite your tongue, Miss Katrina! I happen to be very much in love with my Charles."

Katrina patted Lady Susanna's hand in contrition. "I do apologize. What else did you have in your reticule?"

"Well…" Lady Susanna seemed reluctant to answer until she all but burst out with her answer. "A small but cherished stack of Halfpenny Marvels." Her bottom lip slipped between her teeth as if expecting a scathing reprimand from Katrina.

A grin threatened, but Katrina quelled it. "You mean those sensationalistic little serial books?"

"Good God." She groaned. "It sounds so lurid when you say it like that!"

Katrina swallowed what would surely be looked upon as an insulting bark of laughter. "Lady Susanna—are you truly afraid that people will find out you enjoy reading?"

The girl shook her head. "It's not that at all. While I admit reading for a woman isn't very fashionable at the moment, it's *what* I read that the *ton* won't understand. If they found out, I'd be ruined socially and my husband would never forgive me for it. You see, my Marvels aren't at all the thing." She sighed wistfully. "But I do so enjoy a juicy detective story."

Lady Susanna launched into a detailed version of one of her Marvels, while Katrina's mind wandered. She imagined Jimmy would likely give up waiting for her at some point—and that would mean she'd have to make it back to the Den alone. Again.

Chapter Seven

"Pardon the unsolicited inquiry, sir, but didn't I see you at the Frosts' ball not a quarter-hour ago?"

Jimmy's first impression of the man's question raised significant suspicions, but the sincerity in the friendly manner with which it was delivered sent another message all together. He saw no harm in answering so he blew out a lungful of smoke. "I was."

"Tell me, how well do you know the woman with whom you last danced?" Then he pressed his lips together and drew on his cigar.

"You mean my sister?" Jimmy smiled inwardly. So, this chap had been observing him, eh? Probably some runner from Bow Street. Well, he'd get no information this night.

The man puffed out a laugh accompanied by cigar smoke. "Do you always hold your siblings so closely?"

"I'll give you that." He shrugged and lifted the cigar to his mouth. "She's a beautiful woman."

"I won't argue with you in that regard. I'm just curious about her—where she comes from, why she left so abruptly."

He turned to fully face the stranger and tossed the half-finished cigar into the street. The glowing orange end exploded and smoldered out. "I wonder, though, what is it *you* want of her?"

"Nothing untoward, I assure you."

"Mmm," Jimmy answered, his disbelief ringing in the wordless retort.

"Like you said, she's a beautiful woman."

Jimmy didn't answer. And whoever this fellow was didn't matter. Jimmy wasn't in the habit of spilling narrative about anyone involved with the Den.

"Well, the night is young. I'll be on my way, then."

Jimmy watched the man depart in the same direction from which he'd come. He lifted his hand to his chin and scratched. If Katrina ever got a look at such a fellow, he'd lose her for sure. At once he froze. His free hand went to his empty wrist.

"Well, bugger me. The bloke lifted me dance card!"

"Jimmy!" Katrina called out as she hurried across the street. She'd seen *Mister Nosey* pass by and waited a good two minutes before venturing forth from her hiding place.

He looked up. "Where've you been? And who the hell is that?" He indicated belatedly to Susanna.

Katrina heard the intake of breath from behind her. She stepped up to Jimmy and spoke before he could issue any more expletives. "This is Lady Kendrick. She's a new friend of mine." Susanna caught up to and stood next to Katrina. "Lady Kendrick, this is Mr Lock."

Susanna made to take a step forward. "How do you—"

"For chrissake, Katrina! A *lady*?"

"That will be enough, Mr Lock. Lady Kendrick needed some assistance. It seems her reticule has gone missing. I was wondering if perchance you picked it up *by mistake*."

Jimmy looked as if he was going to throttle her. Instead he threw his hands in the air. "Unbelievable. No, I don't have the bloody thing."

Susanna groaned from next to Katrina.

"Well, did you see anyone else there tonight? Perhaps someone with whom we are *acquainted*?" She tilted her head toward Jimmy to make him understand her meaning.

"No," he spouted with more force than necessary. "It was only you and I. Which is how it should be *right now*. Get rid of her ladyship and let's be off."

Brave little Susanna spoke up then. "Oh, please, Miss Katrina. Please don't send me home without my reticule! Mr Lock," she turned to him. "I will make sure you receive a fine reward if you'll help me locate it."

Jimmy sighed and dragged his hands down his face. "All right, all right. Far be it from me to turn down free money. A friend of mine and Miss Katrina's *did* show his face in the crowd, however brief." He shook his head as if he still couldn't believe it. "Brenner. Heh, it seemed he'd gotten there even before we did. Checkin' up on us, I'd imagine." Jimmy said mostly to himself.

Susanna's eyes widened. "Oh, thank heavens. Perhaps we can—"

"There's no way in hell you're takin' this one to meet Brenner," Jimmy commanded.

Katrina sighed and closed her eyes. There had to be an alternative to taking a member of the elite to the Den. She paced a few steps in the opposite direction. Other than chance of risking exposure, the solution to this mess had to be elementary. If she were to simplify the situation, all she had to do was go to Mr Brenner and merely ask if he had the reticule—but how to do it without Susanna trailing along? She turned to look at her unlikely companions and returned to the spot she'd vacated a moment or two before.

Katrina smiled. "Jimmy?"

"Whatever it is you wish to ask me, the answer is no. I've been served that sweet tone before from women and it's always ended badly."

"Oh, come now. I was only thinking—" she took a tremulous breath and forged ahead. "If you could stay here and watch over Lady Kendrick—"

"Just what do ya think I am, a nanny?"

"Well, I can't think of a better way, can you?"

"Yes, we drop the subject and go home."

Katrina took another step toward him. "Please, Jimmy, do it...for me?" She looked directly into his eyes and watched as his cold façade melted away.

"May the saints preserve me," he murmured.

"You have my deepest gratitude." Katrina rose up on her toes and kissed him on the cheek.

"Well... I hope you don't expect me to entertain the wee kitten."

Susanna's intake of breath didn't go unnoticed. "Jimmy, be nice." She turned to Susanna. "Lady Kendrick, perhaps it would be best if you waited back across the street. You could have a seat in that garden again. I'm sure you will feel more comfortable there than standing on this street corner."

She nodded and Katrina took her by the arm. They crossed the lane and Katrina whispered, "You'll have to excuse Jimmy. He really is a good chap once you get to know him."

"You must know him quite well," Susanna said without looking at Katrina.

"Not as well as one would think," she mumbled back. There just wasn't time to explain her association with the infamous Jimmy Lock.

Moments later, Katrina hurried by on her way to the Den. "I'll be back as soon as I can."

"You owe me a favor, Katrina," he said loud enough for her to hear. And if he had anything to say about it, it would be a favor of an intimate nature.

He grinned to himself. He reached up and touched his cheek where she'd kissed him. It was as if he could feel her soft, warm lips still pressed to his skin. Katrina could talk him into just about anything — even playing governess to a member of the *ton*.

Jimmy glanced at the house behind which Lady Kendrick now waited for Katrina's return and wished he'd not discarded that cigar he'd been given earlier. He scanned the street in front of him in hopes of retrieving the unused portion when a familiar voice caught his attention.

"Drop something, Mr Lock?"

It was Brenner and two of his burly bodyguards, Artie and Oliver. Jimmy wondered if they'd crossed Katrina's path. "No. Just takin' the air."

"Where is Miss Katrina, then? Did you leave her at the party?"

Relief broke the keen hold anticipation had on Jimmy. Obviously, Brenner hadn't come across

Katrina. "Mmm, she was onto something big," he shrugged, "so I broke off early."

"I'm glad I found you alone. I'd like to finish our discussion."

Shite, so this was the reason Brenner peeked in on us earlier in the evening. "Which discussion is that?" Jimmy knew perfectly well—in fact, he'd expected Brenner to not let the subject lie for long.

"You. Wishing to leave the Den."

"Funny, but I was under the impression this conversation was closed."

"Far from it." Brenner tilted his head toward Jimmy.

At once Brenner's thugs took hold of each of Jimmy's arms, making it impossible to get at the knife inside his coat sleeve. He knew it would be futile to struggle so he remained still, but ready to bolt if given the chance.

"I can't let you leave us."

"Can't or won't?"

Brenner thought for a moment. "I suppose it doesn't matter which. Either way, you belong to me—to the East Side Den of Thieves."

"As I told you before, I belong to no one."

"That's where you are wrong. All I have to do is turn you in."

"And be incriminated yourself? I don't think so. Your bluff has been called, Brenner."

Brenner took in a deep breath through his nose. "Well, that's that then. Oliver, Artie."

A beefy fist buried itself deep into Jimmy's gut, inciting a whoosh of air that rushed from his lungs. Another hit smashed into his nose right between his eyes. The pain nearly crippled him—the sound of crunching bones and feel of gushing liquid rolling down his throat and chin were enough to make him want to wretch. His legs gave out, but still Brenner's boys held on. When they released his arms and began to batter his limbs with blunt objects it was all he could take. Jimmy sank to the ground. A knee connected with his left cheekbone and several more foot blows landed in various places on his torso. Shards of light smattered amidst the black oblivion that swirled beneath his eyelids. He accepted it with a grateful heart until his head was lifted by his hair and his battered body hoisted up. His eyes drifted open and he met Brenner's gaze head on.

"I can't have you working for anyone else, you see, so myself and everyone else will just have to accept your death as a necessity."

Brenner drew back his arm. Just before Jimmy blacked out, he saw something sharp flash in Brenner's hand.

Proud of herself for finding the Den via an improvised new route, Katrina made sure that no one witnessed her as she made her way up to Mr Brenner's room. His door remained wide open and a single lamp wick glowed low as if it hadn't been doused properly. She raised her fist to knock upon the portal frame when she noticed the room was unoccupied. With one more glance down the corridor, she stepped inside and turned up the wick. The illumination allowed her to see clearly the few items upon his bed—she was sure they'd come from the Frosts' ball. A single reticule sat in the center of pile of trinkets.

Peeking inside, she espied a stack of papers. "Thank God," she murmured and shoved the bag under her neckline, down into the fabric of her left sleeve. She shook her arm until the bundle fell comfortably to the back. After a quick inspection of each puff that encircled both upper arms, there seemed to be no visual difference between the right and the left. A creaking board sounded from the hall. Her blood froze in her veins. But after a few moments, when no other sounds permeated the silence, she expelled her breath, reached over and turned down the lamp. "Must have been the rafters settling." Relieved, she deftly stepped toward the door, anxious to make her exit undetected.

No one lurked in the corridor — and for that she was grateful. The less trouble she got into from the hierarchy, the better for her health. She couldn't imagine what would happen if someone caught her appropriating spoils she wasn't entitled to.

Not two steps down the corridor, she heard hushed voices. Fear crippled her lungs once again. Slowly she backed away from the noise and headed for the back stairs.

Katrina sighed in relief. In just moments she'd made it back down to the streets and alleyways of London. Not long after, the corner on which Jimmy was supposed to be waiting came into view. But Jimmy was nowhere to be seen.

Chapter Eight

Katrina could have throttled Jimmy. *Where in hell is he?* She stormed across the street and toward the house behind which she'd told Susanna to wait. She whipped around the corner and slammed directly into Susanna.

She reached out to steady the girl. "Good heavens, Lady Ken—" Katrina's tirade came to a skidding halt. Susanna was trembling. "What happened?" Katrina held tight to her shoulders and, regardless of the darkness, tried to look her new friend directly in the eyes to determine just what was going on. "What's wrong?"

Susanna's lips quivered open, then shut before any words passed between them.

"Lady Kendrick... Susanna? What is it?" Katrina gave her a shake.

At once, Susanna collapsed into her arms, gasping. "Oh, you poor dear. You poor, poor dear," Susanna murmured in between sobs.

Given a million years, Katrina still wouldn't have been able to guess what on earth Susanna was going on about.

Katrina drew in a breath to enquire when Lady Kendrick raised her gaze to Katrina's. "I'm not quite sure how to tell you this, but your friend…"

"Yes?"

"Mr Lock…"

"Yes, go on."

"Has been…" Susanna heaved in a ragged lungful of air. "Has been murdered."

"Murdered?"

Susanna's head bobbed up and down at a frantic pace. "Yes."

"What do you mean *murdered*?"

"Murdered. Killed. Good heavens, there is only one perfectly clear definition of the word."

"Yes, of course — but… But *how*?"

"Three men. Two of them beat him and the last one stabbed him. Then they dragged his body off in that direction." She pointed toward the street where not far beyond lay the Thames.

Katrina's world tilted. Susanna thrust out her arm and caught her just before she toppled over. Katrina accepted Susanna's comforting embrace as her thoughts wandered to Jimmy. Tears filled her eyes and her heart ached as if a hole had been carved in her soul. Never once had she fancied herself in love with him, but the twinge of guilt she felt for not reciprocating his feelings nagged at her. He was a dear boy who didn't deserve such an end no matter his circumstances.

"Poor Miss Katrina," Susanna cooed and patted her back. She pulled away to look into Katrina's eyes.

"Now, in my estimation, it isn't wise to tarry here any longer... Who knows if those brutes will be back?"

"Did they see you?"

"No, but we really should depart as criminals often return to the scene of a crime."

Katrina managed a nod and not moments later, allowed Susanna to lead her in the opposite direction of the Thames.

The reality of Jimmy's death refused to take root in Katrina's mind. She remembered snippets of conversation and all the stolen moments she and Jimmy had spent together, aside from when she had learned to steal of course, pondering, philosophizing... He had often made her laugh at a time that should have been the most painful of her life. He'd comforted her and soothed her — she considered him her best friend, regardless of his flirting.

And now he was gone. The only reliable man she'd known in her life. It just wasn't fair.

The night air had turned cold, damper than usual at this time of year, which intensified the chill on her cheeks owing to the trail of tears from her grief. She wiped her face with the backs of her hands and found that she and Susanna had arrived at the portico of a town house. She'd cried the entire way there, and hadn't realized it. Mourning had a way of blurring the passage of time unlike anything else. The amber-colored glass shade mellowed the otherwise glaring gas flame that hung from the ceiling, casting a warm glow about the porch.

Lady Kendrick turned to her. "Again, I'm terribly sorry about your friend. Why, tonight's horrible episode didn't even result in finding my reticule."

Katrina detected in her voice a mix of disappointment and sorrow.

"Oh, yes. Forgive me." Katrina sniffed. "I found it. I just didn't have the opportunity to present it." She shoved her hand inside her neckline and from inside her sleeve she pulled out Susanna's reticule.

First Susanna clutched the bag to her chest, then felt for the contents. "I could hardly believe when it first disappeared. Now I can hardly believe it's back!" She opened the drawstrings and peeked inside. "It's there. It's all there." She sighed. "Thank you."

Katrina could tell the young girl reined in her joy for the sake of Katrina's unhappiness. It was very refined of her to do so. She took a step toward Susanna to voice her appreciation when the words seized in her throat.

"What the hell is going on here?" a man growled and stepped from the shadows.

Even without a visual, Katrina knew exactly who it was. *Shite. The nosey bloke must have been following us!* He either didn't have a life of his own—which she found near impossible to believe owing to his masculine, handsome features—or he was the busiest body in all of London.

"Good heavens, Maxwell, you scared the breath out of me—and I've had quite enough of that tonight, thank you very much."

Katrina flinched. *This man is Susanna's brother? Oh, God.*

"You have a damn fine lot of explaining to do, young lady." He took Susanna by the arm.

Before Katrina could consider bolting, her upper arm was seized as well. "Miss Katrina." Maxwell looked her up and down, likely accessing if she held the wherewithal to escape.

Bollocks, he knows my name.

"And yes, I know your name."

"But how — ?" The mindless query slipped unheeded from between her lips.

"Oh, no. Not until I get the story — the *true* story of why you two have been traipsing around London all night long."

Susanna huffed out an irritated sigh. "I must protest, Maxwell. Ladies, myself included, do not traipse."

"The hell you don't."

"Your foul language isn't helping matters, either. I've never been able to stomach your bursts of temper."

"Don't even try to change the subject, *Stinker*. Now out with it."

Stinker? Ah, yes. The overbearing, older brother. Katrina had heard of such, and this man's portrait could have resided in every shop window in London accompanied by the title.

"Unhand me first. Your violent reaction isn't seemly for a gentleman."

He released Susanna, but not Katrina, then led them both through the front door and through the first portal they came to. The room was dark, save for the blade of light coming through the curtains across the expansive floor. It smelled faintly of pipe tobacco, leather furniture and old books. His hand was like an iron band about her arm, but it was the heat radiating from his body that drove her to distraction.

"Light a lamp," he ordered his sister.

Moments later, Susanna struck a match. "I think the wick needs to be changed, it's nearly done for."

"No time, just use what's left."

"Very well, and stop barking at me like a wolfhound."

Katrina ignored their sibling banter. *My word but he smells nice.* She drew her bottom lip between her teeth to nibble upon it...and to have an excuse to breathe through her nose. His light, spicy cologne reminded her of something—something dangerous, but she couldn't place the incident in her mind.

Once the wick fibers were lit, he demanded of Susanna, "Now. Tell."

"Well, it all started last week—"

"The abridged version, if you please. Start with tonight right after you left to speak with your husband about staying behind at the Frosts' ball."

"Oh. Well, Charles gave me his permission and when I went to find you, you were absent. Where had you gone, Maxwell? I should be good and angry at you for—"

"Stick to the subject at hand, Susanna," he said in a bored voice.

Regardless of their ongoing repartee, not once did Maxwell's grip loosen around Katrina's arm. He was apparently a man who liked being in control. She barely quashed the wayward visual that floated through her mind of other ways he enjoyed his control, but not before it threatened to topple her. Katrina turned her focus on Susanna and realized it would take a lot more than a change of subject to ignore Maxwell.

The lamp sputtered and the flame burnt dangerously low—dangerous because she didn't think she would survive standing so near this gorgeous man surrounded by the intimate cover of darkness. As it was she could sense the pulse beneath his skin, hear every breath he drew. She needed to mask her feelings if she was going to live through this ordeal.

Susanna huffed, pulling Katrina from her thoughts. "It wasn't two seconds after that I realized my reticule had gone missing as well. Miss Katrina was kind enough to assist me in reclaiming it."

"Is that when you two went tearing through the streets of London?"

Katrina started when he turned her slightly so that she faced him—her eyes had adjusted to the dimness and his handsome features could be seen clearly, just like the day she'd left him calling after her on Lovat Lane. *A fist full of pound notes says he didn't like that one bit*, she smirked to herself. She lifted her chin in defiance. She'd be damned if she would give him the satisfaction of her side of the story, even if he was gently kneading the flesh of her arm. Pity the action enhanced her awareness of him by tenfold instead of causing her to want to recoil.

"While Miss Katrina went to retrieve my belongings, I waited for her. In the interim, I witnessed someone—" she paused just quick enough that Katrina understood Susanna's desire not to divulge what wasn't necessary, "receive a beating. The thugs hauled the body away and I haven't seen any of them since."

Katrina shut her eyes as a wave of sorrow washed over her.

Maxwell scoffed. "You sound like one of your Marvels."

Susanna inhaled audibly. "Don't you make fun of my Marvels, Maxwell Courtland! Marvels are intelligent reading, I'll have you know."

"Yes, well, thanks to them, it seems your intellect has acquired the disposition to run wild."

"You don't believe me, do you?" Susanna's voice rang incredulous.

"Let's just say there are a few gaping holes in your version of what happened after you left the Frosts' ball tonight, not to mention the *reason* for your departure—and in an opposite direction to your own home." He then spoke to Katrina. "Do you wish to add anything to this tale, mouse?"

Katrina's gaze shot to his. *Mouse? Was that some sort of slight?* She considered her options carefully before she spoke. She refused to crumble under his scrutiny—why, he'd know in a second how his magnetism affected her. *And how odd to be attracted to such an imperious, ogre-ish male.* It wasn't like her at all. "I wouldn't string ten words together to accommodate your insulting demands."

The ends of Maxwell's lips curled up to display a sinister grin that made the hairs on Katrina's neck stand on end.

"We'll see about that."

"I don't have time for games, Maxwell, and neither does Miss Katrina. I'm sure she needs to get home sometime before the sun rises."

"Oh, you'd be surprised."

Utterly flabbergasted, Katrina tensed. "How dare—"

"*I* will escort Miss Katrina home," Maxwell said with finality.

"The hell you will…"

Susanna cleared her throat. "Now, Miss Katrina. As Maxwell's sister, I can vouch for him that he'll assure you safe passage to your destination. Even though those thugs are long gone, it's still a good idea for him to act as your escort."

Katrina glared at Maxwell. "I can get along just fine without your *brotherly* attentions, thank you very much."

There was that damned grin again. It had appeared just before the lamp wick snuffed out completely. Katrina feebly tried to escape by bending at the elbow, but was thwarted by his unrelenting grip.

"Inasmuch as I'm sure you can, I'm not going to risk it. I'm going to take you home whether you like it or no." Without looking at Susanna, he spoke as he ushered Katrina toward the door by her arm. "Lord Kendrick arrived just before I did. I would imagine he's upstairs awaiting his wife at this very moment. Goodnight, Susanna."

Before Katrina could think of an excuse as to why she was more than capable of getting home by herself, she and Maxwell were outside Susanna's town house and standing at the curbside.

Maxwell's shrill whistle caused Katrina to cover her ear with her free hand. "Was that entirely necessary?"

At that moment, a smart landau with two matching greys pulled up to the gate.

"As a matter of fact, it was," he murmured and threw open the door for her. "Get in."

Chapter Nine

Before a single muscle twitched in her legs, Katrina's feet left the ground. "Hey! Why bother to instruct me when you're already hoisting me into the cab?"

Maxwell was less than a step behind her when he pulled her down to the bench inside. "Now. Where to?"

She folded her arms across her chest in defiance and pressed her lips together.

"I've slept in this carriage before, so it makes no difference if you choose to stay the night here with me or not."

Jerking her chin to the opposite window, she still refused to answer. *Who does he think he is, Prince Albert?*

"Although, it could get rather cold. We may have to share each other's warmth."

"Lovat Lane," she snapped. The street was quite a-ways west of the Den, but she wasn't about to tell him that.

"Ah, yes. That's right about where I lost you last time," he said as if amused.

Katrina couldn't help the grin that tugged at the sides of her mouth. So that's why he hadn't let loose of her—he was afraid she'd dodge him a second time. *Smart man.*

"But I promise you, *that* won't happen again." So much for his jovial tone. "To Lovat Lane near the warehouses, Martin," he hollered to the driver and slammed the door shut.

Neither of them said a word until the carriage turned onto Lovat Lane. When the carriage came to a halt, Maxwell broke the silence. "You must allow that this particular location so near to the docks is rather an odd place for a young lady to live."

"I shan't allow it. Where I live is none of your business."

"I'm afraid it *is* my business."

"How so?"

"Once you claim an association with my sister, your entire being becomes of interest to me."

His innuendo sent an invisible tremor down her back. Katrina took a steadying breath. "I would think Lady Kendrick's associations would be her husband's concern."

"But he's not here, is he?"

"Well, neither is she."

A silence fell between them in the cab. Katrina almost smiled again. She had him this time. *Now to get through the carriage door without him following me.* "Our impasse only proves to me that my departure is upon us, so please move aside so I can go home."

"I cannot, in good conscience, let you leave this cab in the dark of night on some obscure street in the midst of a rough neighborhood."

"Ha. I've seen worse neighborhoods."

"Have you? Where? When? Certainly not in Cricklewood."

Katrina fisted her hands. Bantering with him wasn't getting her any closer to the Den. "These points are moot. What matters is the here and now." Looking out from the windows beyond the carriage, she scanned the area. "You see, there is no one about, so what lies beyond can hardly be considered rough. Then again, there's always a chance that I might be accosted by a particularly hungry alley cat." She moved toward the door when he blocked her with his body.

"Madam, have the men in your life been too feeble to stand up to you, to tell you right from wrong or point out when perhaps your very life might be in danger?"

She narrowed her eyes at him. "Are you implying, sir, that my male influences do not stand up to your masculine standards?"

"That is exactly my suggestion."

A flash of Jimmy's face rushed through her mind, striking a melancholy chord within her. At present, or at least up until this evening, Jimmy had been the only effectively positive male in her life. And she was sure no one on earth could have been more concerned for her safety and comfort. God knows her father never had the disposition to have a beneficial impact on her life. "Don't you dare insult my friends. I'll have you know I've circulated in society where every single man showed the utmost concern for my care," she lied. "In fact, I don't think you'd last a moment were they to examine your dubious intentions."

"Is that a challenge?"

Laughing, she tossed her head in a devil-may-care way. "It matters not what label you apply to it, but I assure you, you would not prevail."

With a flick of his wrist he opened the carriage door and she made to step out, but he stopped her once again. "I will wager that it won't be long until you need a man, a *real* man to save you."

"That's where you are wrong. Not all damsels are in distress. Some of us can take care of ourselves."

At least ten heartbeats pounded loudly past her ears before Maxwell allowed her to alight. Once free of the cab, she headed for the nearest alleyway. Katrina felt the urge to look back. Was he watching her? Was he following her? Did he care as much as he let on? If pressed she'd be obliged to admit how wonderful it might feel to have a man such as him be so concerned about her welfare. But the idea was impossible — and no good could come of wasting time dreaming about that remarkable and unlikely circumstance.

Katrina filled her lungs with damp night air and decided not to concern herself about whom Maxwell Courtland did or did not care for.

Once Katrina rounded the first corner, she hurried in the direction of the Den, yet unawares as to whether Maxwell had followed her or not. By the time the door shut behind her, she was convinced she'd made it all the way by herself.

The Den seemed alive with activity. Her fellow thieves slunk in and out of corridors, conversation and laughter seeped from every alcove — it was like a dimly lit society matron's parlor instead of a secret hovel.

"Ah, Miss Katrina." Mr Brenner sauntered over to her, having just peeled away from a group discussion about who knew what. "I've been anticipating your return."

Her smile felt as forced as it probably looked. "Yes, well —"

Brenner took her by the arm and led her away from the others. "Let's see your share of tonight's take." His gaze shifted to the right then to the left of her, then he grinned snake-like, as if he knew something secret about her that he was disinclined to reveal.

Relieved that he hadn't asked her to share his bed again, Katrina reached into the top of her gown's bodice and pulled from her stays the item dear Jimmy had given her to hold. She handed it to Mr. Brenner who held it up to the light of an oil lamp.

"About Mr Lock—" she began.

Staring at the piece, Mr Brenner brought her statement to a halt with a shooing wave of his hand. "This is a *very* good piece. And you need no longer be concerned with Mr Lock. He will not be returning to the Den." He tucked the bauble into his pocket and focused his attention on Katrina. "He informed me just the other day that he would be leaving us. *Permanently.*"

"But—"

"The subject is closed. I would much rather discuss…" His voice trailed off as his gaze dropped to her décolletage.

Warning bells went off in Katrina's head as Brenner slithered his hand around her lower back.

"Pardon me, sir. I'm looking for the man in charge."

Katrina whipped around to find Maxwell glaring at her and Brenner. *Oh God. Brenner is going to murder me.*

"Who the hell are you and how did you get in here?" Brenner barked and pulled away from Katrina. He made to reach into his coat where he kept his bludgeon when Maxwell stopped him with his words.

"My name is…" he paused but only for a moment. "Court. I'm looking for a job. I followed one of the boys in here, hoping to find work."

Katrina could have choked. *Doesn't Maxwell know thieves are a dangerous lot?*

"This isn't a workhouse, old cocker. Which boy did you follow in? Point him out to me."

Maxwell glanced around. "I don't see him now. Please, sir. I'll do any sort of work, learn any trade."

Katrina opened her mouth to let lose a scalding tirade but shut it just as quickly. *What the hell is Maxwell thinking asking Brenner for work?*

"We don't exactly earn a livelihood here. We take our income from others who can afford to share." Brenner looked him up and down. "You don't seem at all as if you are suffering the ill effects of the streets."

"Well, it's all rather new. You see, I've just divided and sold the last of my property. Everything is gone, including my funds...and my relatives have disowned me. I—I used to gamble, you see."

"Fallen on 'ard times, eh?"

Brenner's smug bravado astounded Katrina as did the fact that he believed Maxwell's bold-faced lies.

"Why should I allow you to stay? What could you possibly have to offer? I should have you killed because you are privy to the whereabouts of my little empire."

"I—I still have my connections at White's—I could get you in."

Katrina watched Brenner's eyes glaze over. "White's," he murmured. "Now *that* 'as possibilities." He placed his hand over his heart. "I've only dreamed of obtaining entrance to such places. Why, one night at White's could be worth at least two weeks' pilfering."

Katrina squeezed her eyes closed for a moment in effort to block out Brenner's dramatics.

"Tomorrow night is the busiest night of the week at White's," Maxwell added to sweeten the deal.

Brenner snapped out of his musings then he slapped a hand onto Maxwell's shoulder. "You may call me Mr Brenner. And provided you are able to deliver what you've promised me, we will come into some sort of an arrangement. But in the meantime, consider this your home... At least until you escort me into White's tomorrow night. And don't even consider reneging. I'll be sure to have my boys alerted to your brief *holiday* here with us."

Maxwell merely nodded and Brenner grinned like a Cheshire cat. "Excellent." Brenner turned to go but paused at Maxwell's next words.

"Where shall I sleep?"

A mere second passed before he answered. "Miss Katrina, show Court to Mr Lock's old room."

Katrina's lungs emptied of air when Brenner offered Maxwell her friend's room. He walked past Maxwell and murmured something she didn't quite hear.

Maxwell turned to Katrina. "I'll just have Miss Katrina here keep me company."

Katrina felt her eyes widen at Maxwell's audacity. *Unbelievable.*

Brenner laughed then, the echo reverberating to the rafters. "I don't run a brothel here, Court. However, I am, on occasion, a sporting sort of fellow myself." He looked Maxwell up and down with a silly grin on his face. "Just so you know, that egg's a hard one to crack," he said tilting his head toward Katrina. "If you can get her to spread her thighs for you, then she's yours. For tonight." He turned and disappeared down a darkened hallway still tittering.

In one instant, Katrina's choices went from a small number to even fewer. Her stomach felt as if someone had punched her and she pitched forward.

Chapter Ten

Max shot his hand out and caught the mouse before she toppled over.

The second her wherewithal returned, she gripped his arm hard and began babbling. "Why did you—? When—? How dare—"

"Perhaps, Miss Katrina, we should have this conversation in the privacy of that room Mr Brenner spoke of."

"But—but you can't just—"

"I'm afraid I did. Now, where is this room?"

Seeming to gather her wits, Katrina glanced around. At once she released him, pivoted on her heel, stormed down a corridor and up a flight of stairs. Max followed her across a catwalk and through a dark doorway. She promptly stripped off her gloves, tossed them onto a small table, lit a lamp, turned the wick up and crossed the moderately clean room to slam the door shut.

"You shouldn't be here," she finally said.

"Neither should you."

"*I* happen to live here."

Max closed the distance between them. "I am well aware, but I want details."

"Details?"

"As in *why* you are here."

Katrina retreated a step. "That is none of your affair."

"Regardless, I intend to find out."

She wagged a finger in his face. "Ever since I met you, I knew you were the busiest body I'd ever come across." Then she lowered her arm as if she were finished with her reprimand. Sadly, this wasn't the case. "Now you've really gone too bloody far. Curiosity is said to have been the demise of certain nosey felines. Just who do you think you are?"

She glared at him, likely expecting an answer to her grating query, but what made his heart sink into his gut was how damned adorable she was. It took almost all of his willpower for him not to smile. "The fact of the matter is that you don't fit in here."

"What Goddamned bloody business is that of yours?"

Hm. Perhaps she needs another swat or two on that sweet bottom of hers. "Aside from your rough language—" Her gaze raked the ceiling, accompanied by an irritated puff of air, but he continued. "Your refined manners for one thing. Your fair skin, the sparkle in your eyes, the way you carry yourself—none of these things say to me, 'street urchin'. And that, Miss Katrina, is only the beginning of my argument as to why you don't belong here."

Katrina turned away and stomped to the other side of the room. She placed her hands on her hips and spun back toward him. "And just where do you think I belong?"

Max's shoulders relaxed. Her reaction proved he'd been right on at least one account. "In a feminine parlor having tea." He took a step toward her. "Playing cards with your friends to while away the afternoon." He inched forward. "At a ball of your very own." Two more steps and she would be in embracing range. "Making appointments with a dressmaker, purchasing fine fabrics and lace with which to adorn yourself."

She dropped her hands to her sides. He could've sworn he saw her chin tremble just before she raised it in defiance. Her voice was soft when she finally replied. "I — I no longer require any of those things."

"I find that hard to believe — and not just because of the feigned indifference behind your words."

The silence that fell between them vibrated with life. The thoughts in her mind must have been whirring at an alarming rate.

Max placed a hand on her shoulder. "Where are your parents?"

Katrina swallowed. Her barely audible voice seeped out, "Dead."

"For how long?"

"Long enough," she breathed.

He pulled her to him, and much to his relief, she permitted the embrace. Her shoulders shook silently. She may have been weeping in his arms, but he couldn't be sure as she uttered not a single sound. His heart went out to the poor girl. She was alone and afraid, whether she'd admit it or not. The fact that she'd survived the streets of London was a testament to her strength — a characteristic unheard of in a good many society women. Not that her fortitude was a flaw, but Max had the means, not to mention the desire, to fix every wrong thing in her life. Perhaps this was the very reason he'd followed her, been obsessed with her since he'd come across her in his study.

Conversationally, he had no idea where to go from here. "I'm sorry about your friend, Mr Lock."

Regardless of how good his strong arms felt around her, Katrina pulled away and wiped at her eyes with the backs of her hands. "I can't believe he's gone." She hated mourning. Hated the crying that accompanied it. The helpless pain was more than she could bear — even when her wretched father had died it'd felt as if she'd never find joy again.

"Was he very dear to you?"

Katrina nodded. "He was." She sniffed daintily.

The room fell silent once again, which applied a numbing whitewash over her sadness. She truly wasn't interested in Maxwell's opinions of her friends and, with certainty, didn't wish to be questioned about every move she made by some man — even one so pleasing to look upon. She'd mastered a continued existence in the last few months without asking people's permission. But then again, how long would she last without Jimmy's help? He'd been her salvation a time or two and now...

"Do sit down, Miss Katrina, and we can talk about it."

Her gaze met his. "I'll sit, but please note that I am disinclined to discuss my private life with you."

"Why? Do you have something to hide?"

Katrina's bitter laugh wheezed from her throat in a single pant. "Look around you. The people with whom I associate wouldn't exactly appreciate my frank disclosure."

"I don't want to know about them, I want to know about *you*."

He did sound sincere, but something in the back of her mind held her willingness to participate at bay. "I don't report to anyone regarding my life."

"Nevertheless—"

"No. I refuse to concede. Why don't you just retire for the evening?" She waved toward the bed. "And forget about garnering any information because you will fail." She made for the door, but he scooped her up off the floor.

She tried to free herself. "What madness—? Let me down!" She scraped her fingers at his shirtsleeves but to no avail. In a flash he'd pulled her down to the bed. Instinct caused her to draw her legs and arms into a fetal ball. Holding tight to her limbs, she felt him stretch out behind her.

"Relax, mouse. You have nothing to fear from me."

"I've heard that too many times to count—and stop calling me *mouse*."

"You are a mouse."

She flipped over so that she was nose to nose with him. "I am not a mouse. I don't even remotely *look* like a mouse." The volume of her voice rose to drive the point home. "So stop calling me *mouse* this instant!" *Insufferable man.*

To her amazement, Maxwell reached out and kissed her on the nose.

"Ack!" She pushed herself to a seated position and scrubbed at the offended spot with the back of her hand. "What did you do that for?"

"I think that for the duration of my stay, every time you disagree with me I'm going to kiss you." He grinned up at her from the bed pillow.

She averted her gaze from his sensual lips that curled up so invitingly at the corners and his appealing dimples that dented his skin beneath each prominent cheekbone. "Why don't you save your games for someone who enjoys your kisses?" She swung her legs over the edge of the bed, intent on leaving the room altogether, but froze at his next words.

"What, you don't think you'll get any pleasure from kissing me?"

She stiffened her spine at his impertinent comment. "Certainly not," she shot over her shoulder. The fact was, she'd probably lose herself entirely while in his intimate embrace, but it was certainly not something one wove into polite conversation. Or any conversation, for that matter.

"Hm. Then I think I'll kiss you each time you lie to me as well."

She turned to glare at him. *He couldn't be serious.* "That wasn't a lie."

"Indeed it was."

"I beg to differ."

"Tell me then. How can you be so sure if you like my kisses or not?"

"Well, the kiss you just slapped onto the end of my nose wasn't exactly a lark."

"I didn't specify where I'd kiss you."

Katrina drew an indignant breath through her nostrils. "You. Go. Too. Far." She rose halfway to remove herself from the bed when, from behind, his arm caught her around the waist.

"Release me!" Suddenly she was face down on his lap, her corseted stomach pressing into his thighs. This scenario was all too familiar.

"On second thought, I think I'll give you a swat each time you lie."

"Are you insane?" She tried to wiggle away, but he held her steady. It seemed like mere hours ago that she was in this exact same position with that man who—

She felt a scraping at her heels as he divested her of each shoe. "What is your last name?"

"I—I refuse to answer! Ha! That's not a lie, either."

Maxwell flipped up the fabric of her gown. "No." *Whap!* "But your remark does qualify as a disagreement."

Katrina yelped when the hit landed. However, when his palm lingered where the slight pain remained, a sensual warmth spread from her stomach to her limbs at the intimate touch.

No. This couldn't be happening again— "Don't," she choked out and tried to push herself up from the submissive position.

"Then answer the question."

He smoothed his hand over her posterior only to follow up with a loud snap in the very middle of her bottom. With a loud exhalation of breath, her eyelids fluttered closed and she stilled, her heartbeat thudding loudly in her ears. Heaven help her, but Katrina wanted him to do it again.

"Your last name if you please."

She pressed her lips together.

Whap! Whap!

A low moan whispered in the back of her throat as he drew tickling tracks over the deepening sting. She became aware of just how much pleasure she found in his wicked game the instant her bottom tilted ever so slightly as if in search of more.

"Harwood," she whimpered.

Maxwell strummed the pads of his fingers over her backside. "Good girl." He slid his hand between her legs.

She sucked a breath of air through her teeth and her back arched of its own accord. She hadn't meant to make such a show, but she felt an urgent need to give his fingers better access to her body. Her reward came when he found her clitoris. He pressed circles into it a few times then drew back just enough to sweep at her soaked, cotton-covered opening.

"My God you are wet," he murmured then continued as if they were having a civilized conversation. "Where were you born?"

Katrina managed to shake her head.

He drew his hand away and she braced herself for the next blow.

Whap! Whap! Whap!

"Ah—Wales!" she panted.

"Good. Open for me."

Her body obeyed instantly.

"Yes," he hissed. "So receptive to my touch." He dragged the palm of his hand from back to front, teasing her. Exciting her. Her breath rushed in and out from between her lips in soft pants.

"Why are you here with these thieves?"

Katrina didn't want to talk. She wanted him to lay her out on the bed and stroke her properly.

Whap!

"Please," she whimpered.

Whap! Whap!

"Ran out of money," she rasped.

Whap! "I didn't hear you."

"God," she panted. "I ran out of money," she said louder. "I had nowhere else to go. Mr Brenner found me and took me in."

He rewarded her by lightly dragging his fingertips over where he'd swatted her. "Good girl. You've had enough punishment. For now."

Maxwell pressed his fingers between her trembling thighs. It felt like Heaven.

Katrina's mind spun in twisted harmony with the pain-pleasure of his naughty ministrations. She floated in a pocket of still, warm air, unconcerned with the world around her.

"Now to worship you," he said just above a whisper. He turned her over and positioned her bottom on the edge of the bed, and removed her drawers and stockings. She barely heard what he'd said when suddenly he pressed his lips and tongue to her already wet flesh.

What in the – ?

Maxwell moaned and the question shifted from a demand to rhetorical as it faded from her consciousness like a mist.

There was nothing in her memory equivalent to the feeling of his mouth on her pussy. The world tilted and the muscles in her legs tensed. Air rushed into her lungs as she anticipated the sweet culmination that was so close she felt as though she were balancing on a balustrade.

"Come for me," he murmured and lapped rhythmically at her clitoris with quick, hard flicks of his tongue.

She sang her ecstasy so loud she was sure she'd hurt his ears. Keeping her poised upon the euphoric crest, he eventually lessened his movements and she floated back to earth.

He nuzzled her mound and inhaled through his nose. "God, your taste... Your scent." She could hear the rapture in his voice and for the first time in her life she felt beautiful. Her boneless body seemed to dissolve into the mattress. Involuntarily, her eyes rolled to a close and she and this glorious man lay there in that position, for several bliss-filled minutes.

Maxwell Courtland. She sighed to herself.

She sat bolt upright and shoved his head from her lap. *What the hell had she just done?*

Chapter Eleven

"What's wrong?" Still engulfed in a musky fog — and with a cockstand as hard as an iron hitching post pressed into the waistband of his trousers — Max gritted his teeth and sat up next to Katrina.

"You can't just walk in here and — and *seduce* me like that!" she exclaimed as she tried to cover her legs with her skirts.

Her face was flushed, her eyelids heavy. Her short hair reached out like dozens of feathery tentacles. She was as mad as a hornet and as cute as a daisy.

"It's a little late for that declaration, don't you think?"

"How typical to question me in such a way after what you did."

Max couldn't help but grin. "Would you have preferred flowers and a calling card?"

Katrina lifted her chin. "Perhaps."

Another evasion of the truth, but he'd let it lie for now. "Admit it. You enjoyed what I did to your body." It didn't matter how she answered. He already knew. The evidence still moistened his lips and clung to his senses.

"You are base. I don't have to listen to this. I am going back to my own cot, *without* you. And there's not room for two, so don't even think about following me." She began to scoot off the bed.

"I'm not going to let you leave this room, Katrina." Max closed his arm around her waist. He pulled her back against his front and held on tight.

She was right, he admitted silently. He hadn't exactly treated her with the respect she deserved. But then again, his instincts had already informed him that she wasn't the type to desire an indifferent, hands-off courtship.

"Release me. I am not some sort of toy."

"True." A rush of electricity surged through his body. He buried his nose in the back of her hair and inhaled. *The real toys would have to wait until later.*

"I said let go of me."

His answer came in the form of his other hand, which he slipped around her middle to completely encircle her. "I promise not to take any more liberties with you tonight if you stay with me until the sun rises." He didn't allow her to answer, but continued speaking. "What time is it? Nearing four, I would imagine."

"Why? Why should I stay with you? You're not exactly a shining example of a host, you know."

He chuckled. *Right again.*

"If you don't answer me—" she warned.

"You *will* remain here with me for the rest of the night. Now you have my answer."

"Bully," she murmured.

Max smiled.

Well, this bed *was* much more comfortable than her small cot. And at least Maxwell didn't do what Brenner did to her. Brenner had awkwardly kissed her with his cold, wet lips, unceremoniously stripped her of her clothes, taught her the names of body parts that polite society never brought up and poked her between the legs until his prick broke through her maidenhead. Then he came on her belly and told her what that meant as well — an orgasm. He told her she hadn't had one because she didn't know how. For all the world, she couldn't understand what all the uproar over coupling was about. It was irritating, uncomfortable and rather brief — the latter she'd been thankful for while she stomached Brenner's company.

At least she thought so until Maxwell introduced her to pleasures that suited her far better than what Brenner had to offer.

However, this sort of thing should never again happen between her and Maxwell. There could be nothing between them. His associations with the upper crust of society, of which she was sure he had, only proved her theory. Besides, she wasn't some sort of trollop who panted after men, for heaven's sake — even men who knew what she wanted before she knew she wanted it.

The recollection of Maxwell's mouth between her legs invaded her thoughts and Katrina relaxed against him. In lieu of almost every one of her already few options being taken from her, and regardless of her wanton abandon this evening, she felt Maxwell was, at the very least, on her side. She claimed friendship with his sister, after all — that alone should secure an alliance with him, provided it returned to a more *abstinent* state — and he overlooked her chosen profession.

Feeling more tranquil, she pointed her toes and stretched her legs upon the bed.

His seduction of her person could be blamed entirely on him. For one thing, she hadn't initiated it. Hell, she hadn't even been given a choice.

Maxwell is terribly wicked. She yawned. *Susanna is so sweet, but her brother… Her brother could probably seduce a woman at twenty paces…*

* * * *

Katrina had no idea how long she'd slept. Only a small amount of light leaked in through rifts in the walls near the high ceiling. The lamp on the table burnt low — she'd forgotten to douse it last night. *Jimmy's lamp.* The memories mercilessly rushed back to her. *Poor, darling Jimmy.* Pain tore at her heart all over again, then the familiar fear began to seep in. Who would be her champion now?

A noisy sigh came from behind her. She froze. So that was the warmth at her back. The *nefarious* Maxwell Courtland.

In order to keep her sanity and not get intimately tangled up with him again, she needed to get off that bed, out of that room, and fast. Ever so slowly she pulled away. First her shoulders, her back, her bottom… His hand slid away from where it sat so intimately upon her hip. She moved her foot toward the edge of the mattress —

At that moment, he moaned in protest and recaptured her by the waist. She rolled her gaze to the ceiling as he pulled her to him, helpless against his physical strength.

He sighed and seemed to melt into her once more.

Was he still asleep? Could she try again after a moment? The sun had risen and he had, after all, promised she could go at that time.

Hadn't he?

Maxwell inhaled and the vacuum of air tickled the hairs on her neck. She reached up to scratch the spot. He kissed her knuckles and actually chuckled, as if he had a secret.

She retracted her hand and pushed out a breath hoping it sounded as exasperated as she felt. "Are you quite through?"

"No," he whispered. "I haven't yet begun."

"The sun has risen. You are honor-bound to keep your promise from last night."

"Mmmm…" He held her tighter. "Let me taste you again."

Katrina lost her breath. "You can't be serious."

"I don't think I've ever been more serious." His voice was a mix of groan and growl in opposition of his words.

"No. Absolutely not. I'm shocked you would even ask—No, I refuse your request." Somewhere in the back of her mind she knew Maxwell could force upon her whatever licentious act he desired. Why, he could bind her to the bed and— No! She held fast to the last shred of willpower she had, even though the visual that flashed before her sent heat rolling over her skin.

He had the audacity to chuckle again. "Come now. Indulge me."

One more whispered invitation like that and she'd succumb for sure. "That does it." She tore away from him and scooped up her stockings, drawers and shoes from the floor. Just because he was big and strong and seemed to care for her didn't mean she should follow her desires like some primate in the jungle.

"Do not flee, my lady Harwood."

She spun to face him. "What? And sit here only to listen to your depraved suggestions?" *Because I won't be able to refuse you much longer. Wait... My lady Harwood?*

At once Katrina realized that not only had he drawn from her this new interest in and craving for unusual pleasures, but he also knew certain things about her that she'd kept secret for months at the Den. *Shite.* In addition she'd practically fallen into an affair with him like some desperate widow. *Well, this stops here and now.*

"You will allow me to leave or... I'll—I'll tell Brenner on you."

Maxwell clasped his hands and placed them behind his head. "What would you tell him? That I want to pleasure you?"

Oh, God. Her knees went weak. After an indignant intake of air, she retorted. "No, that your name really isn't *Court* and that you lied to him."

"I didn't lie. Court is the first half of my last name, and I *will* get him into White's tonight."

"Do you have any idea how dangerous these thieves are?"

"I do. Do you?"

She stomped her bare foot. "Don't be ridiculous. Of course I do. I live here, remember?"

"Were you aware that Brenner had Mr Lock murdered?"

What? Katrina dropped everything, reached out and held onto a nearby chair. "No," she breathed her protest, as her mind whirled with the possibilities. Come to think of it, she wouldn't put anything past Brenner. But still.

"How could you possibly know such a thing?"

"Before we retired to this room last night, I heard him murmur something as he passed me."

She thought back to when Maxwell had first met Brenner. "I don't recall—"

"He didn't say it loud enough for anyone but me to hear. In fact, I'm quite certain he was talking to himself."

"What did he say?"

Maxwell sat up. "Something to the effect of, 'Poor dead Jimmy'. I heard him tell you Mr Lock left, not that he died. Susanna merely said he'd been beaten, it was you who informed me that your friend had been murdered."

Katrina stumbled forward and lowered herself to the bed. She buried her face in both hands to cover the pain that surely showed there.

Jimmy's sly grin flashed before her closed eyes. His young life had ended in violence and Katrina felt the loss keenly. She wept mutely, allowing the emotion to undo her at last. And for a long time, Maxwell stroked her back without uttering another word.

* * * *

They'd been sitting there for at least an hour if not two when Katrina heard Maxwell's stomach growl and her own hunger reared up to greet his. She hoped Jimmy wasn't watching her mourn from above. He never had allowed human weakness to interfere with his own life—and he'd likely scold Katrina for her tears. With shaking limbs, she pulled herself together and spoke, "Thank you for your compassion, Maxwell. I need to change and then we should eat."

"Yes. Of course."

She stood, re-gathered her discarded clothing and paused at the door. "It will be difficult for me to face Brenner after what you told me."

Maxwell was right behind her. "You will have to pretend you know nothing, for no other reason than to keep yourself safe. In the interim, I could do some investigating into Mr Lock's murder. Perhaps I can find evidence against Brenner."

She turned and looked up at him. "How in the world would you do that?"

"Well, I could begin with a search at the local funeral parlor."

"That's very kind of you, but do you even remember what Jimmy looked like?"

"Oh. You may have a point."

"Besides, what could possibly be done to convict his murderer?" She opened the door with her free hand.

"You would be surprised how efficient Scotland Yard's Criminal Investigation Department can be in that respect." Then he whispered, "Especially if we could procure the murder weapon."

"Very well." She nodded and they crossed the catwalk to the stairs.

* * * *

Thankfully, no one else occupied the small kitchen area. She joined Max after she had changed into a simple ivory day dress with embroidered lilacs down every other stripe. She looked charming as she buzzed around the table like a bee.

"Your suit is completely rumpled," she commented and handed him a piece of bread dipped in berry jam. "I doubt if you'll get across the threshold of White's looking as if you've slept in your evening clothes."

Her observation drew his attention to his attire. "I don't suppose you have a butler service here?"

A tinkling laugh brought his gaze to meet hers as she took the seat across from him. "I don't think you'll find a single flat iron for miles. Hot *or* cold."

"So what do you suggest?" Max bit into the day-old slice of bread and chewed while Katrina tapped her perfectly kissable lips with an index finger.

"There's nothing for it. You'll have to change before you take Brenner on his *dream* outing." She glanced down at her heel of bread and slid it toward the center of the table, as if at once uninterested in the bland fare. And rightly so. He set his bread down as well.

"What if his men are watching the doors?"

Katrina sat up a little straighter and whispered. "I found a corridor not three weeks ago that had at least an inch of dust on the floor, indicating that no one had ever used this particular passage. I may have been an awful thief, but I'm an ingenious sneak."

Mice usually are. He kept the thought and the grin that accompanied it to himself. "Shall we, then?"

She nodded and stood.

Max glanced about to double-check they were alone, which they were. "I think we should also call at the funeral parlor." He hated to bring up the subject, but knew eventually that they'd at least have to touch upon it. "Are you up for such a morose excursion or would you prefer to wait a day or two?"

He watched something akin to pain pass over Katrina's features. She then lifted her chin. "If it will help convict Bren — the murderer, then I'm all for it."

His chest squeezed in sympathy for her, making it difficult to draw breath. He took her by the hand. "Your bravery does you credit."

"I'm quite sure it's merely a shell of courage, but it's all I have left."

* * * *

His mouse had avoided the guards by taking them through the isolated, cobweb-strewn corridor, the clever girl. Once they were well away from the Den and strolling along the streets of London blending in with the crowd, Max suggested they visit the funeral parlor first as it was on the way to his town house.

Her hand trembled in the crook of his arm as he reached for the doorknob. He glanced down at her. "You are sure?"

She nodded and they stepped into the parlor. A bell attached to the back side of the entrance sounded, announcing their arrival. Max closed the door behind them and detected a faint stench of decay in the air. Aside from the smell, it seemed a normal yet mostly unfurnished parlor, save the two caskets on display at the far end of the extensive, narrow room. Light streamed in through the muslin under-drapes, but the space still seemed dark — must have been the fact that it was permanently dressed for grim occasions. It was likely only those who'd recently lost loved ones that visited.

A man entered through drawn velvet curtains beyond the caskets and walked sullenly down the long floral runner toward them. "Good day, I am Mr Timothy. How can I be of service?" His unruly salt and pepper hair conflicted with his perfectly tailored suit — which denoted his profession — but his cheerless smile was entirely accurate.

"Please excuse our intrusion, Mr Timothy. My name is Mr Courtland and this is Miss Harwood."

Mr Timothy nodded a solemn bow and Max continued. "An acquaintance of Miss Harwood's has gone missing. She is under the suspicion that he's passed on. We were wondering if anyone has been brought here to be prepared for burial whom you've yet been unable to identify."

"I see. Was it Atwood, Elfman or Hendrickson who sent you?"

"I beg your pardon?"

Her voice had been barely audible, but Max understood Katrina's confusion. He suspected the three chaps Mr Timothy mentioned were affiliated with Scotland Yard. If that were the case, he and Katrina's snooping about might be just a tad premature.

"Pardon my assumption, Miss, but everyone in the industry knows I take in the strays — I mean *unidentified* bodies."

Max relaxed somewhat. Not wanting to appear altogether uninformed, he jumped in, "No. We chose your establishment because... Well, just consider it a lucky guess."

"Remarkable. As luck would have it, I've got two males what come in early this morning and one left over from yesterday 'round noon."

"Would you mind if — ?" Maxwell tilted his head toward Katrina.

"Not at all. I'll just go prepare a few things. If you'll permit me."

"Of course."

Mr Timothy turned and headed for his workroom.

Max waited for the velvet curtains to close behind Mr Timothy then he turned to Katrina. "I'm afraid you will have to summon whatever courage you have left, my dear," he said softer than a whisper.

"W—what do you mean?" she replied, matching his tone.

"We must be very careful. If you act in response to your friend's corpse, showing any emotion whatsoever, both of us will be called upon for questioning by the authorities—and I need a bit of time to find suitable evidence against Brenner. Can you pretend it's not Mr Lock even if it is?"

Katrina swallowed hard. "I shall do my best. But why then did you give Mr Timothy our real names?"

"The last thing we want in a circumstance such as this is to be caught fibbing about our identities."

"And if they catch us lying about the body, what then?"

"We'll just tell them... You were too distraught or some such. We'll have to deal with that at a later time."

She nodded once, catching on like the astute girl he knew her to be.

The curtains parted. "We are ready for you now, Miss Harwood."

Katrina glanced up at Max. *We?*

Chapter Twelve

The second they entered into the room where the bodies were kept, Katrina began to gag. From his pocket, Max handed her his clean handkerchief, the stench causing his own eyes to water. The tiny space allowed no ventilation—no open window, not even a hole in the roof. One shelf-lined wall held dusty glass bottles in different sizes of clear and not so clear fluids. It was enough to make the stomach roil.

"My apologies. I've been working here for so long one might say I'm used to the smell." Mr Timothy, now covered in a black and white pin-striped bib apron, chuckled and reached for the corner of the sheet on the first corpse. With a flourish he peeled the cover to just below the dead man's chest and peered at Katrina.

She quickly looked away. "That's not him," she murmured from behind the handkerchief.

Mr Timothy nodded and moved on to the next body. With the same sort of show, he revealed the bloated face of the next cadaver for her.

Katrina winced and averted her gaze. She shook her head.

Max felt as if he could no longer stand upright in the room. He himself lifted the third covering and tossed it back down just as quickly after Katrina rejected it. He took her by the elbow. "Thank you, Mr Timothy. You've eased Miss Harwood's mind considerably," he said as they broke through the velvet curtains.

"Call any time. We're here most every day."

Mr Timothy's voice faded fast behind them as they hurried for the front door.

Once outside, they both drew in mouthfuls of what fresh air London afforded, trying to purge themselves of the stench and taste of decay and embalming solution.

"Definitely not the way to spend recreational time," Max panted, trying to lighten the situation.

"How does he do that day in and day out?"

"We will never know. Some people are just cut out for that sort of occupation."

"By the way, none of those corpses where Jimmy," she said with a painful, distant look in her eyes.

"I didn't think so, either. Come." Max offered his elbow and together they headed in the direction of his town house.

* * * *

The second they turned down Hamilton Place, all thoughts of how beautiful she felt strolling along on the arm of Maxwell Courtland vanished, and Katrina began to worry. She'd pilfered, or at least tried to pilfer, from a house on this very street not three nights ago. Was Maxwell the victim's neighbor? Had that woman noticed her diamond earrings were gone and raised the alarm in the vicinity? Did she linger even now on the street in search of them? Katrina peered down the street. Mercifully, no one was about.

Maxwell paused at the foot of a brick pathway—at the exact property that deeply concerned her. She peered at him and almost thought she saw a smile curl the corners of his lips.

"Is something wrong?" he inquired.

"No!" she replied much louder than she'd wanted to. Contrary to what she wished to believe, she was a dreadful liar when taken by surprise. She cleared her throat. "Why?"

"Nothing, really. It's just that your steps have slowed ever since we rounded the last corner onto Hamilton Place."

"Oh," she said in way of apology.

Maxwell started forward once again. He placed his hand on the iron latch and her breath caught. Tossing the gate wide, he escorted her through.

Shite.

Inside the breezeway, Katrina glanced around, trying not to appear frantic.

She felt her blood thicken when a butler appeared, but Maxwell waved him off. "No need, Simmons. I've got this one." Without missing a step, the man departed and left them alone in the corridor.

Katrina felt a single drop of perspiration inch its way down between her shoulder blades.

Maxwell took her by the hand and drew her up the main staircase. He paused only briefly on the first landing. "Look familiar?"

"What?" She nearly jumped out of her skin.

"Does my home look familiar to you?" he asked and continued on to yet another set of stairs.

"I—I'm sure I don't know what you mean."

He chuckled and led her through a set of double doors to a spacious, very masculine bedroom. "Indeed you do. You attended my ball earlier this week."

"I—I— *Your* ball?"

"There's no need to pretend otherwise. It's all behind us." He gave a bit of a smirk.

How odd, she thought, that he hadn't cared that she'd nearly pilfered a good deal of his silver that night.

"Honestly, your attendance is irrelevant. However…" His voice lowered to an intimate level. "That was the night you got your first taste of my hand upon your bottom."

Katrina choked and set her cool fingers upon her burning cheek. She should have scolded him right then and there for remarking aloud about her penchant for his rough play, but now that it was out, and just between the two of them, it didn't seem so upsetting. She dropped her hand to her side. Could it be that he was truly a trustworthy man or did this sense of trust come from the carnal sport they'd shared together?

He stopped in the middle of the room, turned and pulled her close. "Can I tempt you with any other pleasures, Katrina?"

She looked away. It wasn't even noon yet and her thoughts could have easily drifted to… Her gaze landed on an open door off to the left of the huge four-poster bed and the sizable porcelain tub that lay therein.

"Oh," she breathed.

"Ah, yes," he murmured, having obviously followed her line of sight. "Would you like to take a bath while I pack a few things?"

"Could I?" She despised the audible desperation in her voice, but if it got her into a tub of hot water, she didn't care if she sounded like a braying donkey. "I would like nothing more in the world."

"Very well. Come."

Maxwell brought her in to where the tub stood on four golden claw feet and showed her how to work the matched plumbing. He retired from both chambers and in no time, Katrina was up to her chin in luxurious hot water.

* * * *

Contented and pruned to her toes, Katrina, wrapped in a large drying towel, cautiously peeked into the bedroom from where she'd soaked for who knew how long. She expected her clothes to be lying on the bed where she'd left them, but they weren't there. She quickly scanned the room. They weren't hanging on the privacy screen in the corner, they weren't draped over the chairs near the fireplace, and neither did they lie atop the fainting couch beneath the window. If this was some sort of joke Maxwell had made at her expense, it wasn't remotely funny. She promised herself that she'd wait only a few minutes longer before sounding some sort of alarm out of the door and down the hallway.

Drawn to the focal point of the room, Katrina inspected the huge four-poster. The deep burgundy brocade bed covering matched the velvet curtains perfectly, but then what else did she expect? Maxwell was a wealthy man. He could likely afford a change of linens and draperies for every day of the week.

On the bedside table sat an iron-bound leather chest. The box looked similar to her father's tobacco and pipes house—but that couldn't be what it was. Maxwell didn't smell of pipe smoke. In fact, he smelled cleaner than any man she'd ever stood next to. With a glance in the direction of the door, she pushed aside the bolt and lifted the lid. Strangely shaped items set deep in black velvet grooves met her gaze, including a few pen-shaped items that were far too wide to be writing implements. She leaned in to take a closer look and found that they were shaped quite like—

"Oh, good heavens." Katrina placed her hand upon the lid to slam the chest shut when a sheer white organdie drawstring bag holding a strand of green beads caught her eye. "What on earth...?" She reached in and drew out the bag, dumping the bauble into her hand. The thumb-sized, perfectly shaped stone balls clacked against one another. The beads were green jade and smooth and in between each lay a knot in the sturdy thread that shone like oriental silk. She held them up by one side, her gaze roving up and down the long strand.

"And they say I'm curious."

Katrina was sure that for a second her feet had left the floor entirely. "Who says that?" she all but yelled and made to lower the beads back into the box.

"Well, *you* for one." Maxwell took the beads by the opposite end and draped them over her shoulder.

"Busybody. I said you were a busybody." The strand slipped through her fingers and he caught it.

"And the definition of a busybody is...?" As he waited for her response, he dragged the beads back and forth over the muscles between her neck and shoulder.

Her eyelids fluttered shut. "One who can't mind his own business."

"Someone who is nosey?"

"Yes," she whispered, reveling in the feel of the beads as they thudded across her strained muscles. It almost tickled, but was strangely soothing at the same time.

"Someone who rummages through another's possessions?" he whispered.

"Mmm." Maxwell trailed the beads to her décolletage and back and forth across her skin. Her entire being relaxed and her head lolled backwards in utter rapture, only to rest upon his shoulder behind her.

The strand acted as a necklace as he tied it in place. "I want to show you something, Katrina." His voice floated by her ear like a breeze.

Maxwell gently took hold of her hands and placed them up behind his neck. "Interlock your fingers."

At his suggestion that was more like a breath than words, she did as she was told. Slowly her drying towel slid open, then down her body to rest upon the floor. Maxwell began plying the beads to her skin again, this time running them over her bare chest. She inhaled and held her breath as the strand rippled over her nipples. Back, forth and across, she arched in invitation for him to continue. The beads delighted her with a buzzing pleasure she found utterly delicious.

She was nearly out of breath when the strand rolled down her belly and over each hip.

"Spread your legs just a bit for me."

Katrina took one step to the right. She opened her eyes wide when the cool beads came to rest between her legs. "Maxwell..." She unlaced her fingers and her hands came to rest at her sides.

"Shhhhh... Shut your eyes, Katrina. I'm not done yet."

She swallowed and did as she was told. Slowly he began to draw the beads up over her clitoris. When he reached the end of the strand, he reversed the action. Katrina whimpered as the jade rumbled over her sensitized skin, shaking her with wicked vibrations.

Her breathing became heavy, her body strained to reach the exquisite orgasm she knew awaited her with the next pass of the beads. Her eyelids fluttered open for a second and she glimpsed Maxwell on his knees watching as he worked the beads over her body with a look of both carnal knowledge and awe.

He sped the slick beads over her faster and faster, the zipping sound of the strand demanding she take her pleasure now. She cried out in an ancient song of ecstasy and came. At once Maxwell pressed a finger up inside her, sending even more pleasure to her core and shock waves over her body.

"Beautiful, absolutely astounding," she heard him declare as she pitched sideways to take hold of the nearest post. How was it that he was panting as hard as she? He removed his hand and the beads and helped her recline upon the bed. He stepped over to the wash basin but returned quickly. Just how he'd gotten undressed so fast she'd never know.

As Maxwell drew a cover up and arranged it around them just so, her body trembled with the after affects his naughty beads had had on her. She'd never heard of such a thing in all her life. But, God, how she'd enjoyed it.

"Katrina," he murmured, still out of breath.

"You don't have to say a word. Just take me."

"Oh, God, Katrina." Maxwell's voice sounded like the harsh whisper of a dying man. "How desperately I've wanted you." He shifted to hover over her, cool air stealing under the covers where their warm bodies had created heat, and placed himself between her legs. He sank the full, hard length of him deep inside her. Her inner muscles accommodated him and clasped at the width of his cock. He made to draw out and she bore down on him so as not to allow it. He groaned. "So unbelievably tight." He doubled his efforts and as if her body knew instinctively what to do, her hips rose to meet his, establishing a primitive rhythm that reverberated to the depths of her soul. He'd pleasured her with the beads and now her insides were being served the same indulgence.

Without missing a beat, Maxwell drew one of her legs up so that her knee dug into the side of his ribs. He angled his cock and thrust so hard that she felt as if she were going to shatter into a million shimmering pieces.

She clutched at his shoulders and held on, taking in his scent and feeling the strength of his body as it crashed down against hers. "Oh… Maxwell…" Was she pleading with him or did she wish to convey her unfathomable joy? There was no safer haven, nor more blissful pursuit such as what he provided. Handsome, strong, kind…certainly knowledgeable in the sexual arts.

When she came, stars exploded behind Katrina's eyes and her body reacted just as intensely.

"Katrina," he moaned. Maxwell's muscles strained beneath her hands, she could feel his orgasm as it hurtled through his body.

With the euphoria she felt coursing through her, she now understood what all the to-do was about.

Chapter Thirteen

"Well, do I look the part?"

"Mr Brenner, you seem entirely well-to-do—impeccably dressed—a member of the elite."

Max and Brenner stood at the side entrance to White's. Max elaborately primped and fluffed Brenner's evening wear, picking imaginary lint from his sleeves, ruffling the jacket fibers to a noticeable softness. The man, thief or no, certainly had a demonstrative regard for the dramatic. "Now, go on in. No one will question you."

"What? You won't be joining me?"

"I couldn't possibly be seen after all that my family has been through," he said, not only with a straight face but managing a palpable concern via his drawn together eyebrows. He was defiantly getting the hang of this.

"And what if they *do* question me?"

"If they ask by which member you gained your entrance, tell them—" A smile nearly blossomed upon his face at his inspired idea. "Tell them 'the youngest man ever to get silk in the history of Great Britain' and that they'll have to wait until the end of the week for the papers to divulge that information." Max chuckled then. "I promise you, they'll be more than accommodating especially after the whispers begin. You'll be the most favored guest of the evening."

"A judge, eh? My, my. You did run in elevated circles, didn't you?"

"We can gloat later, Mr Brenner. Through this door is an entire flock just waiting to be fleeced."

"Right you are." Brenner grinned and Max returned it.

Max's smile faded when the side door to White's shut with Brenner inside. *What a bastard.* He had no doubt the rat would succeed in his dubious efforts that night and into the wee hours of the morning. "Let him do well," Max whispered the wish to the sky. He was certain the contemptible man's end was coming soon, one way or another. *Very soon.*

After walking a few blocks in the opposite direction of White's, Max fortuitously found a hackney waiting to be hired. "To Lovat Lane." No sooner did he take his seat when the carriage lurched forward. *Back to Katrina,* he sighed, torn between elation and agony, *and the hideout of the East Side Den of Thieves.*

* * * *

Max found Katrina standing in the middle of Jimmy's old room.

"They do work fast, don't they?" Her voice was soft, but it echoed off the walls of the barren space.

He came to a stop next to her, aching to put his arms around her. She looked so forlorn in the golden light of the oil lamp she held.

"They've removed everything. Who knows where they've taken it all?" She let go a cold chuckle. "They've even taken his bed."

"What will they do with it all?"

"Sell it. Trade it. Hoard it. It could be any number of things. All done without regard to the owner. That's how they work, you know. Entirely without feeling."

"You miss your friend very much, do you?"

She sniffed and raised her chin a notch. "I do."

Jealousy coiled around his insides. Did she think of him when he was away from her like she did that *boy*? He cleared his throat. "I was thinking that perhaps we might look for the murder weapon."

"Yes, of course."

Even though she'd acquiesced, she didn't move from her spot. Max stood for a few moments while emotions like whispers skittered across her features. At once she took a shuttering breath and turned, inching her way to the door, whispering as she went.

"We must be careful. Follow my lead. Move when I do, stop when I stop. At least until we get to Brenner's room." She lowered the wick so that the lamp flame was nearly out. "This time of night most everyone is out gathering goods, but just in case there are a few lingering—"

There was no need for her to finish her thought. Max fell into step behind her.

In moments they were ascending the half-flight wooden staircase to Brenner's room. They hadn't been seen, but were forced to pause their steps at least twice before entering yet another corridor while Katrina listened for movement.

Once inside Brenner's room, Katrina set the lamp down, turned up the wick, and quietly wedged a chair beneath the doorknob.

"Now, if I recall, Susanna said something about—" She swallowed. "That he was beaten first then stabbed."

"So we are looking for perhaps a bludgeon?"

"Or some sort of d-dagger."

Katrina's voice wavered between strained and helpless. He felt genuinely sorry that she insisted on subjecting herself to situations that brought her pain.

"We don't have to do this now."

She stiffened her spine as if it would boost her fortitude. "Of course we do. It seems everyone is out and Brenner is occupied. There is no better time I could think of to search the premises."

She now seemed near hysteria, the poor darling. "Could we take a moment to gather our wits?"

Katrina sighed restlessly but surrendered.

Max closed the gap between them with two strides and took her in his arms. She tilted her head forward to lean against his chest. He held her close and murmured, "I wish we were in a different place altogether—a different time, surrounded by different circumstances."

He felt her nod again. He couldn't blame her for her lack of conversation. Max pulled away just far enough to place his right knuckle beneath her chin. She tilted her face up toward his when he applied the tiniest amount of pressure. Her eyes glistened with unshed tears. Her beautiful lips looked moist and inviting.

Without thinking, he brought his mouth to hers.

She kissed him back without the slightest hesitation. As their lips pressed together, he reached for her tongue with his and she moaned at first contact. Her hands slid up to cup his jaw. He enjoyed the sensation, wishing she'd wrap herself around him and remain that way.

That did it. He was lost. He lowered them to their knees, to the plush Persian rug beneath them.

He pulled away from her to look into her eyes. "I'm going to bring down Brenner. This I promise you."

"I trust you," she whispered.

His heart soared. Knowing how many times she must have been promised things by the men who had treated her so cruelly throughout her young life, he silently vowed to do everything in his power to prove himself worthy of her trust.

"But how could I ever thank you?"

Max reached down and grabbed a fist full of her skirt fabric.

"We really don't have time for this," she warned.

"Indeed we do, but it will have to be hurried this time," he growled playfully and found the drawstring of her drawers. He dragged the cotton to her knees. In an instant he lay between her thighs and released his cock. She freed one of her legs from the inside of her drawers, spreading herself wide to his impulsive deed. Lust surged through his body, further stiffening his eager rod.

They could be caught. She must know this. But her excited breathing told him she was up for a quick fuck. Hell, she'd barely protested... His sweet, brave little mouse.

He manipulated her clitoris with his thumb and forefinger, soft and fast. She came so quickly it seemed she'd been halfway there before he'd touched her. He shifted, pressing his demanding shaft into her and she drenched him with her cream, her inner muscles greedily milking him while he pumped his hips against hers.

Aside from the fact that danger undeniably played a part in his excitement, the hunger he felt for Katrina was irresistible. To lure this intoxicating creature, and convince her to let him inside her could very easily become his own personal drug. They obviously weren't married, not even engaged, but everything about it felt right, settling into his mind as if he'd been called home from a lengthy absence. He gazed upon her rapturous face, about to speak her name.

"Maxwell—" she whispered.

He came the instant he heard her sweet voice call for him.

In the seductive haze of afterglow, they lay there for a few moments, catching their breath, when Max noticed a lone item—it looked like a small pile of fabric under Brenner's bed. He disengaged himself from Katrina, fastened the front of his trousers, and reached for the object, pulling it from its hiding place.

"What is that?" she asked while hitching up her drawers.

"Don't know."

They moved toward the lamp. It was a small carpet bag. Max pulled apart the handles. Inside sat an expensive, jewel encrusted dagger that still held traces of blood on the slim blade.

Katrina looked away. "Why would someone keep such an awful thing?"

Max didn't dare touch it. "Don't know. A trophy, perhaps? Regardless, it's got to be the murder weapon."

"Agreed," she said, still averting her gaze.

"This bag holds vital evidence—if we're caught with it, the only hope of putting Brenner away will be Susanna's testimony."

"Which would never be enough on its own."

"Precisely. Now we need to get your things—"

"What? Why?"

"Did you think you'd be out of harm's way here?"

"As much as I've always been."

"Which means not at all."

"I'll have you know I've survived on my own since concluding my father's affairs—"

"Be that as it may, you are no longer safe. Once we remove this bag, I'm sure Brenner will interrogate everyone at the Den until he finds out the truth. Where will you be then?" His argument was sound, he reminded himself, but he needed to keep focused so that he would know for sure that he wasn't doing this for his own selfish reasons.

She went still and quiet for a long moment. He had her. Now if she'd only admit it and go without a fight.

"Where, exactly, would I be able to go if not here?"

"My townhouse." The words rolled off his tongue much easier than he'd anticipated.

"Don't be absurd."

"All right then. Where?"

"I'll stay here."

"Out of the question." She made to protest again, but he cut in. "I have servants who will watch over you round the clock. What better protection can you garner other than that?"

"I can't possibly put your staff in danger."

"You wouldn't know this, but both Walters and Simmons belong to gun clubs. They each have an impressive arsenal at their fingertips and would defend my home and those within its walls like mother bears. So I can assure you with great confidence that you will not be putting anyone in danger. And I'm afraid it will have to be an extended stay—at least until we can be assured of your safety."

She gave him a murderous look, but, thankfully, she conceded with a stiff nod.

Katrina removed the chair from in front of the door and they wove through the corridors and hallways to her hovel.

She opened her trunk and stood over it.

"What's wrong?"

"I don't think I want to keep any of this."

"Are you sure? This is all you have in the world."

She shrugged. "Far too many memories attached to these items—memories I'd be happy to put behind me."

"Up to you. However, if you take but a few things, it might give the impression that you've gone far afield."

He watched as Katrina chewed on her lower lip for a moment. "Very well."

She went to her tiny bed and straightened out the top sheet. She then dug through her trunk, pulling out bits of clothing—tossing them onto the bed and making it look like her things had already been rifled through. "I'll take my latest gown. Brenner hasn't even seen this one yet. I hid it so he wouldn't sell it like he has everything else I had of value."

"Like what?"

She moved over to the bed and began tying the corners of the sheet so that it gathered the items together. "My hair," she said coldly and took up the bundle.

His gut wrenched for her as she bravely marched toward the door. He stopped her by placing his hands on her shoulders. "I'm so sorry. But I must say, I think the way you wear your hair is most attractive."

She gave him what was likely a placating smile. He couldn't imagine how Brenner had convinced her to sell her lovely black locks, but he found his stomach burning with even more contempt than before for the bastard. Max embraced her for a moment hoping he conveyed how much he admired her forbearance. "Now, let's get the hell out of here."

As they snuck around corners and through a network of alleys, he contemplated how to present all this to the police without implicating Katrina.

Chapter Fourteen

"So with your permission, sir, I shall begin making inquiries about a second groom tomorrow morning."

"That will be fine, Simmons. We may need an extra maid as well. I'll leave it all to your discretion."

"Thank you, sir." Simmons bowed and left the dining room.

Katrina had merely toyed with her dessert while Simmons came to inform Maxwell that his household was in need of filling a position. She wondered if she shouldn't consult Simmons about finding her a situation with a reputable house—perhaps one with children.

"You don't find the custard to your liking?"

Maxwell startled her out of her reverie. "No," she explained. "It's very tasty. I'm just finished."

He placed his napkin upon the table. "Do you like to read? I have an extensive library in the country, but all my favorites are here in town."

She sat forward. "You mean you have more than one house?"

"Well, it belonged to my parents, really. This one," he gestured to their surroundings, "is entirely mine."

Katrina didn't even want to speculate how wealthy the Courtland family was—certainly more so than her own used to be. "I'm not sure I could concentrate long enough to enjoy a book right now."

"Understandable."

"I think I'll just retire for the evening."

Before Katrina contemplated standing, Maxwell was there, pulling out her chair and offering his elbow. She took it gladly and pondered how comforting his presence was.

On the way up the stairs, Maxwell let Walters know he wouldn't be needing him this evening and Katrina's heartbeat quickened. She knew it would be her playing the role of his butler tonight.

He escorted her all the way to her door. Katrina thanked Maxwell, but didn't shut him out. Instead, she observed him as he made his way across the hall to his room.

He turned to look over his shoulder and caught her watching him.

Her cheeks heated with a fury.

Maxwell spun on his heel and leaned against the wall next to his door. "Personally, I'd rather not be alone tonight. Would you?"

Katrina shook her head.

With a wicked grin, he held out his hand to her. Shutting her door, she practically flew into his arms.

He embraced her, trying to kiss her and bring them into his room at the same time. Once inside, their steps faltered. Max longed for a connection with her as if they hadn't made love in months. Their labored breaths intermingled with each gasp. Their lips disconnected and reconnected as he groped the back of the door for the bolt. Laboriously they peeled each other's clothes off, fumbling and clumsy like a couple of wayward lovers who'd snuck upstairs together at a formal dinner. The room felt warm and inviting — as if somehow granting permission for their promiscuity.

Katrina giggled at the impulsiveness of it all. She'd said earlier that she trusted him, not realizing at the time upon how many levels her trust for him lay.

Maxwell kissed her as if she were his only connection to life. She let him back her toward the bed. Her gaze darted to the wooden box that sat on the table next to his bed, but she turned her head, trying to quell her curiosity. As if she were a feather, he lifted her by her bottom to set her upon the velvet coverlet. It felt cool against her heated skin and her breath caught.

He paused to look into her eyes. "What is it?"

"It's nothing. It's —" Unable to help herself, she glanced at the box.

Maxwell grinned playfully and he narrowed his eyes at her. He must have known exactly what drew her attention. He cupped her cheek in his palm. "I would deny you nothing. You know that."

She nodded. He slid his hand from her face only to capture the back of her neck, easing her closer still to him.

"You trust me, don't you? You know that I'd never hurt you." He briefly pressed his lips to hers, then allowed her to reply.

"Yes," she breathed her answer in a small puff of air.

Without breaking eye contact, he reached out, tossed the bolt aside and flipped open the lid. "We'll start out…small."

Before she could get a good look at the box's contents, he laid her back upon the bed.

"Maxwell—"

"Just stay exactly how you are. Don't be afraid."

Katrina swallowed, ignoring the heat that made her feel as if her body would burst into flames at any moment. She didn't dare try to imagine what he was about to do but was unbelievably excited to find out.

After drawing the curtains over the windows, lighting a single candle and double-checking the lock on his door, he went about placing pillows beneath parts of her body, a cylindrical bolster beneath her neck so that her head tilted slightly back. It wasn't at all uncomfortable, but it did obscure her line of sight from her exposed body. He set padding under her bottom and a cushion underneath each knee, spreading her legs well over shoulder-width apart.

"How does that feel? Are you comfortable?"

Regardless of her racing heart and her exposed state, she managed to respond. "I am."

"Good girl."

Gently he took her arm and set it above her head, but to the side. He did the same for the other. Then something soft and cool like satin slipped around each of her wrists. He fell quiet and she made to lift her hands to see what he'd adorned her with, when she found she couldn't. It was some sort of restraint. A drop of moisture oozed down between her parted legs.

"Maxwell?"

"Shhhh. Don't speak."

Katrina licked her lips. She could hardly keep from fidgeting when a smooth object rolled up one of her legs. She closed her eyes. *The beads. Oh, God.*

The mattress dipped as he climbed on and settled between her legs. "I remember how much you like these," he murmured as his fingers spread her nether lips apart.

The faint scent of olive oil tainted the air. She felt him place the cool, newly oiled strand on either side of her clitoris. Painfully slow, he dragged the beads to one end, then reversed them. All the way up and all the way down he drew the beads along her sensitized, slick skin.

Pure, blissful, throbbing torture.

On one of the passes he paused and she felt a nudging, an inch or so lower than the opening of her vagina. He began to trail the beads again, and after a few passes, the nudging became a gentle intrusion, no wider than a finger.

She squirmed to find a more comfortable position.

"Shhh, you'll get used to it. Just breathe," he said and began again with the beads. This time, he rushed the beads up and down until she couldn't stand it any longer. She came and as she did, she felt him slide his finger into her vagina, and the intrusion widen her anus. She shuddered with delight at the added sensation. Suddenly, he dipped his tongue into her belly button.

It was too much, she felt out of control—she came and came again, unable to contain her moans of ecstasy. The orgasm seemed to go on and on. The higher she climbed, the louder she became. He finally brought her down slowly, gradually softening his strokes. He retreated from her, making a quick stop at the wash basin—the only evidence perceptible was the tinkling water. Not moments later, he climbed back upon the bed and snuggled close to her side.

"Did you like that?"

"It was… I never thought—how magnificent—" She turned to him in an attempt to gage his thoughts. "What about you? Surely you are in need—"

"I am. I wanted to make sure you were pleasured first."

Katrina's gaze dipped to his lips and back to meet his eyes. "Amazingly so."

In a flash he slid inside her, kissing her mouth, drawing orgasms from deep inside her with his insistent cock, wrenching them from her very soul.

Later as she drifted in and out of sleep, Maxwell put the room to rights. He took great care with his 'toys' as he'd called them. He cleaned and dried them, and put them back into the box as if they were the crown jewels.

Carefully he climbed back into bed so as not to wake her. However, she'd not drifted off completely.

"I noticed something, uh…earlier."

"Did you now?"

"Mm. What's through that door?" She indicated a panel in the wall to the right side of the bed. It wasn't a door per se—she could see that it was the width and height of one, but it bore no visible handle.

"Why, you curious little imp," he chuckled.

Katrina shrugged a shoulder and tried to smother a grin.

"Tell you what. Since I've been up for over twenty-four hours and didn't sleep well the night before, we'll save that door for another time, shall we?"

Katrina nodded and snuggled closer still to Maxwell.

* * * *

In what felt like only the blink of an eye, Katrina awoke alone in Maxwell's bed. She sat up, trying to ascertain what the time could possibly be, as only a faint bluish light seeped in between the curtains.

The door to the bathing room opened and Maxwell stepped out wearing trousers and shirtsleeves — much in the same manner he had the morning he'd followed her to Lovat Lane — but this time his hair was wet.

"I'm sorry, did I wake you?"

Katrina, loving the sound of his voice, sank back down and hugged his pillow, rubbing her face back and forth, inhaling his scent. She felt him sit next to her and peeked up at him. "No, but had I known where you were, I'd have joined you," she said feeling an acute shyness that she'd even uttered the words.

He chuckled and bent over to place a kiss upon her temple. "If I could — " He pressed a few more kisses across her cheeks and forehead — "I'd stay here and make love to you all day long. However, there are a few things I need to attend to today."

She sat up. "Like what?"

"Well, for one thing, I want to keep up the pretense with Brenner for just a while longer."

"How do you mean?"

"I must throw him off my scent. I need to make him think I had nothing to do with you leaving the Den."

"And how will you accomplish this?"

He sighed and shook his head. "I'll think of something. In the meantime, I have a request."

Naked, she wiggled out from beneath the covers and sat next to him. "Yes?"

Maxwell groaned and leaned into her, pushing her backwards onto the bed. "God, just look at you." He kissed her, his lips playing over hers like a master at his instrument. "You little temptress."

Katrina giggled.

He pulled her to a sitting position. "I want you to promise that you'll stay in the house — just for today."

"But where will you be? I won't be here alone all day long, will I?"

"Of course not. However, I have a few errands to run. I'll be back by the time breakfast is served. In the meantime, you should probably scoot back to your room. You could sleep for a couple more hours if you wish. I'll have Simmons let you know when to go down to table."

She nodded, but he made her assure him verbally. He took her by the hand. "Promise you will do me this one favor? It will ease my mind greatly."

"I shall." She smiled.

"Good. Now go — before I ruin all our well laid plans and take you back to bed."

Chapter Fifteen

"Where in the hell is she, Brenner?" Max demanded. The bastard's thugs had been waiting for him in the alleys that led to the Den. They'd seized Max and conveyed him directly to Brenner. Now in the presence of the man himself, they still held his arms in an iron grip. Max struggled—not to escape, but as if he were about to murder Brenner with his bare hands. Which sounded entirely too tempting regardless.

Brenner's eyes narrowed. "Strange, but I was about to ask you that very same question."

"If you've hurt her, I'll kill you myself."

"Heh. I got more protection 'ere than the Queen in her bedchamber."

"Goddamn it, Brenner! What have you done with Katrina?"

"Now, Court. Could it be that you managed to crawl between those nearly impenetrable thighs of 'ers and now think you have some sort o' claim on the chit? I must say, she's a fine ride, but I can find a dozen other women much more obliging than Miss Katrina—and who are far less costly to bed."

Good God. Max's stomach dropped. He recalled the conversation he'd had with Katrina about Brenner and how he'd sold almost everything she had possessed that was of value. The bastard must have taken her virginity as well. How else could she have been initiated into this rabble?

"There. You see? Logic wins out over libido eight out o' ten times." Brenner smirked. "I'll make you a deal. You tell me what you know, and I'll tell you what I know. And together we'll find our little runaway and bring 'er back."

Max still detected a hit of mistrust, but went along with what was offered. "All right." He relaxed his stance, and with Brenner's permission, the thugs released him. "The last time I saw her was before I took you to White's. I came back and most of her possessions were gone. I set out to find her but was unsuccessful."

The thief fisted his hands. "It's that boy. She's gone to find him." Brenner suddenly seemed convinced of Katrina's motive.

"Who?"

"Jimmy Lock, that's who. I knew they were chummy—"

"What do you mean?"

"She won't find him... Alive, anyway."

His two thugs chuckled.

"How do you know he's dead?"

"Never mind 'ow I know." He turned to his men. "Go an' search both sides of the Thames—at least three miles up and down. Upturn every lean-to, every 'ovel—in every slum and shanty. Do whatever it takes to find 'er."

As Max watched the men leave, he decided to send the bastard's thoughts in another false direction. "I'm not sure she's one to go that route. I think you and I should search the local whore houses – the ones that cater to a more...*upper*-class clientele." He turned a gaze on Brenner that he hoped looked convincing. "That's where I think she'd hide, not cowering in some shed." Max could practically hear the rusty wheels grinding away in the scurf's head.

"Hm. You're onto somethin' there. Besides, after my take at White's I could use some...*recreation*."

Despite Brenner's casual stance, Max detected that the thief remained guarded – and rightly so. What kind of thief would he be if he trusted a stranger with such unreservedness? "Had a fine time of it, then?"

"Better than fair. An' I did pretty well at the tables, if I do say so."

"Good show." Max smiled wondering which one of his friends had emptied his pockets on account of this charlatan. "I will make arrangements for you to visit Madame Dubois' Salon tonight."

"You know Madame Dubois?" Brenner asked incredulously, eyeing Max with something akin to suspicious disbelief.

"Doesn't *every* gentleman?"

* * * *

Max arrived in the breakfast room just as Simmons was helping Katrina into her seat.

"I've hired a maid for you, Miss Harwood. A Mrs Dillard. She came with excellent references."

"Thank you, Simmons." She turned a dazzling smile on Max that caused his heart to jump.

Recovering from the lightning bolt of joy, he spoke to the butler, "Simmons, I'd like you to ask Susanna and Charles to dine with Miss Harwood and me tonight."

"Of course, sir. Hors d'oeuvres at seven, supper will be served at eight."

"Simmons, you are unsurpassed at your profession."

The butler bowed and departed.

Katrina's soft voice drew his attention from the butler's retreating form, "I should probably take a tray in my room."

Max couldn't believe what he was hearing. "Whatever for?"

Her shoulders seemed to slump forward, all the sparkle disappearing from her eyes. "Maxwell, I highly doubt it would be prudent for *Lord Charles Kendrick*, who aspires to be a judge, to dine with a thief."

No, he wouldn't allow her to think she wasn't worthy of such elevated company. "*Former* thief. And besides, when he hears our plan to bring in Brenner and his affiliates, I'm sure he'll not only find the conversation of interest, but he'll take an instant liking to you as well."

"I'm not at all convinced of that. However," she brightened slightly, "I'd love to see Susanna again."

"Then it's settled." He'd have to let Susanna know that Katrina was in need of feeling as though she belonged here with them. Because she certainly did.

One of the staff entered and served first Katrina then him.

"How did you pass the morning?" he asked, looking to lighten her mood.

"After a hot soak —"

"Your favorite." Max grinned.

"Yes." He observed a blush kiss her cheeks then she continued, "I took your advice and wandered around in your library."

"And?"

"You've quite the collection."

The server quit the room.

"Found it more interesting than the silver, I take it?" Max teased.

He watched a barrage of emotions pass over her features. She finally pinned him with a sly, astute stare. "You're lucky you caught me when you did. Otherwise we'd be eating with our hands right about now."

Her stinging humor cost him a burst of laughter. "You little minx. I've a mind to put you over my knee right here and now."

Katrina briefly glanced over to the door through which Simmons had taken his leave then turned her gaze back to Max. She narrowed her cat-like eyes at him. "You wouldn't."

"I will. The very second I have a lock put on that door."

Her eyes blazed to life and he watched a visible shiver bolt through her.

She was the one — absolutely, unequivocally, beyond a shadow of a doubt — *the* one.

"However, I regret that our naughty little scenario will have to wait until later." It was imperative that he go visit the Madame and set the stage for Brenner tonight.

"Then I suppose I'm stuck with my book."

"For now."

"Where are you off to, then?"

He'd have to tell her later. If he knew her at all, she would probably insist upon joining him at Madame Dubois'. "The locksmith."

She blushed prettily. He did so enjoy the many sides of Miss Katrina Harwood.

* * * *

"Madame Dubois, how lovely to see you again." Max bowed over her hand, but she wouldn't release him when he tried to let go.

"Maxwell Courtland. It's been far too long since you've visited." Aside from a few additional silver strands at her temples, he would have sworn that this woman hadn't aged a day in five years.

"You'll have to excuse the early hour—"

She pulled him closer. "As the unprecedented favorite of mine and my ladies' hearts, you know you are welcome *any* time, day or night."

In his younger days, before Susanna had her coming out, he'd spent a great deal of time and money, both night *and* day, within the many nooks and nests of the infamous Madame Dubois' Salon. "You are too kind. And as tempting as your generous offer is, I have a favor to ask of you—"

"A favor? *Indeed.*" She let loose his hand and slinked across the room, keeping her back to him, her filmy emerald green and black lace peignoir acting like a train on the floor behind her.

Max chuckled. "It's not what you think. And don't worry, I'll be paying you well for what I'm about to propose."

She turned and said over her shoulder to him, "I am intrigued, sir. Care to step into my parlor?"

"Said the spider to the fly?"

Madame Dubois' laugh was throaty, practiced. However, she was never unfair to those able to pay, so in that sense she was a good sort of woman. That, and she could keep a gentleman's secrets as if they were her own. With a flourish of organdie and lace, she turned for her office.

Max dutifully followed, intent on having the entire house of Dubois give Brenner everything he deserved. All night long.

* * * *

Max still couldn't be sure if Brenner was a straight beer drinker or aspired to imbibe champagne or cognac like his betters. And because Max wanted Brenner good and incapacitated, beginning tonight and into the next morning, he arranged to have a case of dark ale, and a case each of French bubbly and well-aged brandy delivered to the Madame's establishment. He let Madame Dubois know that she could keep what Brenner didn't consume, which only sweetened the deal for her.

However, the most excellent element of the arrangement was that she'd promised Max that the toys used on the utterly intoxicated Brenner would be the biggest and the driest they had. Max couldn't help but chuckle at the thought of what would befall Brenner the next morning—too hungover to stand and too violated to sit.

If only Max could devise an additional torture that would impede Brenner from lying down...

Chapter Sixteen

"Let's just say I called in a favor or two with Madame Dubois."

"A favor? Can't imagine what she'd owe you for."

Max shrugged. "Years ago I got her out of a couple of sticky situations with the authorities," he lied to Brenner. His recent inclination to be overly economical with the truth surprised even him. "She was, and still is, *very* grateful."

"You've quite a number of tricks up your sleeve, Court. You're quickly becomin' my new favorite."

Great. Just what I've always wanted. "I am indeed humbled." They rounded the last corner a block from the exclusive establishment. "You remember the rest of the way to Madame Dubois', yes?"

"Could get there blindfolded." He rubbed his hands together.

"Be careful what you wish for," Max murmured. "Now remember, give Madam Dubois your name. Everything you may want is on the house tonight. Don't hesitate to live out your most debauched whimsies."

"I fink I'm gonna' enjoy dis."

"I promise it will be a night for the books, my friend." Max clapped him on the back, ushering Brenner forward.

* * * *

Katrina had felt entirely uncomfortable throughout the meal while Maxwell had enlightened his sister and her husband about certain vulgar realities of Katrina's life, that is, until the moment Susanna placed her hand atop hers just as dessert was finished. "You poor dear," Susanna cooed. "Having to endure the streets like that."

"I must confess…" Susanna's husband took a sip of his wine and continued, "Your bravery outshines any modern lady or gentleman I've come across. Very admirable."

It didn't feel brave in the least. It felt more like survival. "Lord Kendrick, you are too kind." Katrina placed her free hand over Susanna's and gave it a sisterly squeeze.

"Nonsense. And please call me Charles."

Charles' kind gesture made her feel warm and cozy inside. It had been such a very long time since she'd felt safe, secure and appreciated. Katrina nodded and glanced over at Maxwell when he spoke, "So you'd be willing to take the case, then?"

"Good God, yes. To have a hand in pointing out a murderer and foiling an entire ring of thievery…"

"He'll get the silk for sure," Susanna chimed in.

Everyone chuckled.

"Well, my darling, that goes without saying."

"Yes, of course." Susanna blushed.

"I'm up for pounding out a few schemes to corner this chap, if you are, Charles," Maxwell said.

Charles grinned. "Will brandy and cigars be involved?"

They both stood. "I was thinking we'd have tea and cakes."

"I'm so sorry. Would you look at the time?"

Susanna giggled. "What a pair you are."

Maxwell and Charles exited through the door that connected the dining room with the library.

She turned to Katrina. "I swear, the time those two spend in serious conversation pales in comparison to their capering about like a comedic twosome."

Katrina disentangled her hand from Susanna and placed her napkin upon the table. "You are a very lucky woman. To have a husband with such a sparkling sense of humor will keep you both entertained for life."

"Yes, I suppose you're right."

"Come. Let's retire to the parlor and wait for the Kendrick and Courtland show to finish their engagement in the library."

Not wishing to bother the staff, Katrina turned up the lamps on either end of the settee and they made themselves comfortable.

"When you think about it, your life sounds as exciting as a Halfpenny Marvel."

"Only the danger isn't on the next page—it's *real* and just outside the front door."

"Too true." Susanna nodded, then began to chew the inside of her cheek.

"What is it, Susanna?"

Susanna shifted upon the settee. "I..."

"Go on. Whatever it is, I'm sure we can get to the bottom of it," Katrina encouraged.

She watched Susanna's gaze slide away then drop to dwell upon the Persian rug. "I—I suppose it's a confession of sorts."

Katrina placed a hand upon Susanna's arm but said nothing.

"Right then." She sighed and turned back to Katrina. "It's strange how one can feel entirely set on a certain subject, until at once they're thrown into a circumstance where their view is no longer clouded by vanity."

Katrina's expression more than likely showed her confusion because she truly had no idea what Susanna was on about.

Susanna tucked a stray lock of hair behind her ear and continued, "You see, there is something you need to know. I had big plans for Maxwell."

This took Katrina by surprise. She ignored the emotion, not wishing to be rude to her friend. "What sort of plans?"

Susanna forged ahead, "I wanted him to marry, so I put together a list of eligible society girls for him to choose from."

"Oh." Katrina removed her hand from Susanna's arm. Out of the recommendations on Susanna's list, Katrina may have been eligible as far as being unattached, but a society girl she was no more.

"Wait, Katrina, you mistake me. I just wanted to tell you before you heard it from anyone else. I no longer wish for him to marry any of them. I want him to marry *you*."

A huff of laughter escaped Katrina. "I'm afraid that decision is neither yours nor mine. Maxwell will have to decide for himself if and whom he marries."

"That is exactly what he's been trying to tell me. But until now, I guess the message was beyond my silly intellect. I'm not sure why I didn't see it sooner, especially after Maxwell's Spring Ball."

"Why? What happened after the ball?"

Susanna sat up a little straighter. "Now promise you won't take offense."

"You have my word." *Good heavens, now what*? The suspense was slowly killing her.

She nodded. "Very well. You see, the morning after, Maxwell asked me about you."

"*Me*?" Katrina's insides gave a jump. That was the morning she'd lost him at Lovat Lane. Surely he'd been angry with her at the time.

"Precisely. But while we were discussing the candidates on my list, he asked me if I had seen a girl with short black hair the night before. I should have figured out right then and there that he was attracted to you. However, I didn't know you. In fact, I—I made some very harsh judgments against you, even before we met. And I want to apologize. You've been helpful and heroic and besides all your other unspoken virtues, you've turned Maxwell into quite a different man."

A thief, virtuous? Impossible. "Susanna, you're being overly kind with your compliments—"

"Not at all!"

"However, Susanna, my curiosity demands I find out in what way you think I've changed Maxwell?"

"My dear. I've known him all my life, obviously, and I can tell you with the utmost confidence, that he's never been so attentive to one female *ever*. Not even to me. Not even to our mother!"

As frank as Susanna was being, Katrina felt it was Maxwell who'd in fact transformed her into something society wouldn't look at with too much distain. He'd been unprecedentedly kind and protective, not to mention the things he'd shown her about her own body.

"So I don't want you to think for a second, whether I thought so previously or not, that someone else is better for him than you."

Katrina shook her head and smiled. "I promise. And if it makes you at ease, we don't have to speak of it again. You know, I've never had a better friend than you, Susanna." She shifted on the settee and continued, "And once more, you have my deepest gratitude for the spare clothes you brought earlier. Words of thanks seem feeble in comparison to your generosity."

"Nonsense. That's what best friends do, and they keep each other's secrets as well—like my Marvels and your *Den*. But I don't want you to ever be concerned. I'll keep the information locked away in my heart forever."

Not even her family had she ever been shown such forbearance. Katrina was in awe over Susanna's graciousness. "So will I."

"Oh, Katrina!" Susanna dove forward and hugged her so tightly she thought she'd lose her breath. "You know I'd do just *anything* for you, dearest." She heard Susanna sniff as if she'd started crying. Unable to hold back, Katrina, too, felt the flood of tears beneath her eyelids.

"Look at these two. In it up to their knees," Charles said from the doorway.

Katrina looked up to see Maxwell grinning. She disentangled herself from Susanna and stood. "That's how best friends are—quite like the two of *you*."

"What?" Maxwell challenged and strode to the center of the room. "Do you fancy that I chose Charles for Susanna? I needed a companion for bridge and I recruited the first gent up for a gamble to happen by."

Susanna giggled and ran to her husband. "Well you can't have him for cards or anything else. He's *mine*." Then she reached up and kissed Charles soundly on the cheek. Her husband chuckled and gave her a squeeze.

Maxwell gained Katrina's attention. "I'll be up as soon as I see them out," he whispered.

Without hesitation, Katrina bade the couple a heartfelt goodnight and left the parlor. Once in the entrance hall, she flew up the stairs, breathless to find out if Maxwell truly did love her.

"Oh, no, Maxwell," Susanna insisted. "It's cold and damp out tonight. You should send us off here from the door." She reached up on tiptoe and kissed him on the cheek.

"She's right, Max. No need for you to come out. Our carriage is just across the street."

Charles patted the outside pocket of his coat, and nodded, wordlessly telling Max he'd keep the dagger safe until it was to be presented as evidence. Max heard the crackle of the brown parcel paper he'd wrapped around the weapon when they were in the library.

"Very well then. Charles, I'll stop by your office before lunch tomorrow to see to the details of Brenner's capture."

"See you then." Charles nodded his farewell.

Max watched from the doorway as Susanna and Charles' carriage pulled away when a movement through the trees across the street caught his eye. It was Brenner's thugs walking by. Max shut the door, but not completely so that he could peer out through the inch of space between the portal and the oak. The men were talking quietly to each other while they strolled along. It didn't seem as though they'd taken any note of Charles and Susanna's departure, thank God, and neither did they seem to know that they were traveling past 'Court's' house. They moved out of sight and Max breathed a sigh of relief.

However, now that he knew for certain that Brenner had his scoundrels scouring the streets for Katrina, it seemed that her person needed to be looked after even more closely than he'd originally suspected. She'd have to go so far as to stay away from windows until they could round up Brenner.

And he'd have to inform Katrina of Brenner's men's presence in a way that wouldn't whet her natural curiosity nor stir her penchant for danger.

Chapter Seventeen

With her ear pressed to the inside of her door, Katrina listened as Maxwell made his way up the stairs, down the hallway and into his room. She'd had the maid, Mrs Dillard, ready her for bed then, not moments ago, dismissed her in hopes of a late night tête-à-tête with Maxwell. She wore a white, sleeveless camisole and matching short drawers and stockings— a mishmash of items Susanna had given her. This was the first evening in the time she'd spent under his care that they hadn't retired at the same time—and it was about to drive her mad. What if he wasn't in the disposition to see her tonight? What if he thought it was too late an hour? What if he was just too tired?

Katrina pushed away from the door and climbed atop her bed. Every negative scenario that her mind invented seemed completely logical. He was human, after all. She leaned against the stack of pillows at her back and folded her arms across her chest. It would serve her right—she'd been too happy lately, too spoiled. She wasn't worthy of continuous bliss like this. No one was.

A soft knock startled her. "Yes?"

The door opened and Maxwell's face appeared. "You in bed already?"

"Not at all. I was...waiting for you, actually." She couldn't fight the grin that insisted upon turning the corners of her mouth up.

His face simply lit up. "I'm...very glad you did."

"So am I." Her reply was embarrassingly breathless, but she ignored it.

"I—I have a fire going in my room..."

"Oh, yes. Of course." She hopped from the bed, blew out her candle and, after making sure no one was about in the hallway, followed Maxwell to his room.

He shut the door and turned to her.

"I thought tonight went very well. Your sister seemed—"

Katrina didn't get to finish her sentence. He had closed the empty space between them and enveloped her in his arms. She'd barely had time to take a breath when he pressed his mouth to hers. Katrina gave in most willingly.

He kissed her until she was dizzy with it, until the ache between her legs demanded she mention it. "Mmm... Ma... Maxwell?"

He lifted his lips away from hers. "You shouldn't be trying to converse right now, not while I'm trying to kiss you senseless."

Katrina giggled. "Perhaps that's why I'm speaking— I *am* senseless. So, to my knowledge, you've obtained your objective."

"Then talk, and be quick. For I'm not sure how much longer I can refrain from making love to you." His embrace loosened, but just a bit.

"I seem to remember something about you showing me where that led." She indicated the secret doorway in the wall.

"You mean to say that you haven't even taken a peek, while I was out?"

Feeling suddenly very shy, she tucked her lower lip between her teeth and shook her head.

"Hm. That must have been very difficult for you."

"Not at all. I waited because I wanted *you* to show me."

Maxwell stood there for a few endless moments staring into her eyes. Emotions she hadn't seen in him before passed over his features — as if he couldn't believe what she was asking, as if he doubted his ability to acquiesce her request, as if an invisible uncertainty had taken hold of him. Sensing his hesitation, she placed her hand upon his cheek.

"I trust you."

His warm gaze conveyed to her how pleased he was at her admission. She stood there beneath his arousing scrutiny, and mere heartbeats before she was about to throw herself back into his embrace, he led her to the panel in the wall. With his free hand, he took hold of the chair rail molding and pressed a hidden button on the underside. The door popped open.

It seemed as if she was passing *Through The Looking Glass*. With not a spark of perceivable light, it engulfed her in an inky darkness. She stopped a few steps in and Maxwell released her hand. In moments he lit an oil lamp and shut them in. The red glass shade cast an otherworldly glow over the room. Unidentifiable shapes as big as furniture stuck out from the walls. Padded and covered in different hues of leather, a tall slim bench, a short square foot rest, and one furnishing the size of a couch had above them several silk cords that hung from the ceiling. She stepped forward and took hold of one, then noticed the chains that dangled side by side with the slender ropes.

She surveyed the circumference of the small room, and observed a beautiful ostrich feather fan and at its flanks, a few single plumes tacked to the wall. On another side of the room, next to a waist-high bench, which was too high for anyone to sit upon comfortably, hung an assortment of buggy whips and bridles from pegs. She took a few steps toward the odd collection.

"It seems your groom has mistaken this room for the stables."

"What?" He walked over to where she stood. "Ah." He chuckled. "No one knows this room exists, save myself and now you."

"No one? But—" She raised her hand to one of the whips and found that it possessed a wide tab of soft kid leather at its end. She swallowed hard. "Oh, I see." That breathless quality had returned to her voice. She dismissed it as her curiosity overtook the moment. Her heart began to pound out a voluble tattoo. "Then, is this for—?"

Maxwell slid his arms around her waist from behind. "Yes."

She detected that the same breathlessness had assailed him as well. Her gaze darted to each whip. One had fluffy down-like feathers for its end. One possessed a long, soft leather fringe. One had what resembled rough, braided horse hair that seemed more spiky than pliant. There were more, but she could no longer dwell upon them as her simmering blood was now at a boil beneath her skin. She turned in his arms and looked into his eyes, but just as quickly, her aplomb slipped away like a mist. She studied his shoulder as the words echoing in her mind struggled to be set free.

"Maxwell, I—" Katrina drew a shuttering breath. "Would it be possible—?" She cleared her throat. "That is to say, could you—?"

"Yes?" She could hear the slight grin in his voice.

"You aren't going to make this easy, are you?"

"Make what easy?"

No, he wasn't. And she knew that if she didn't exhume the courage from deep within her to ask him this very moment, then she'd never be able to. "Oh, for heaven's sake. Look, I want it." Her gaze darted to his. "I want you to use those horrid little torture devices on my bottom."

"I'm sorry. Wha—?"

"And don't you dare make me ask you again. If you didn't hear the first time, then turn about and we shall leave this room this instant."

She'd never seen such a wicked grin. Her breath became trapped in her lungs. He placed his hand behind her neck and drew her cheek to his. "Whisper your request into my ear."

Pondering his appeal for a moment, she realized that it certainly was easier asking him when he wasn't looking directly at her. Perhaps she'd pass him a bloody note next time.

Katrina turned her face so that his lips brushed the outer shell of his ear. One breath, then two. How in the world could she ask for what she longed for? At once it came to her. Without waiting for a single second more to pass, she whispered, "Spank me."

She nearly lost her breath he hugged her so tightly, but she had to admit, it felt wonderful to be enfolded and safe within his strong arms.

Maxwell began nibbling her neck, placing little kisses up and down the skin there, tonguing her sensitive throat. She clung to him while he stoked her fire. He was oh, so good at fostering within her a great anticipation of what was to come.

Finally he turned her around and placed her in front of the waist-high bench that protruded from the wall. He lifted her arms and wrapped a silken cord around each wrist. He then moved to a small ship's wheel mounted next to the bench that she hadn't noticed before. Turning the wheel to the right made the bench extend farther out from the wall. It pressed against her hips, causing her rump to stick out behind her. She held onto the restraints for balance. At her back, Maxwell nudged her feet apart. Painfully slow, he inched her short drawers over her derrière a little at a time—first a tug on the right side, then he'd tug down on the left, grunting and murmuring naughtily the entire time. "The skin of your arse is so soft." He stroked a tickling finger beneath the fabric. "Oh, the things I want to do to this bottom." She could feel his warm breath caress her skin with each tortuous reveal.

If he didn't lay his hands on her soon she just *knew* she would die.

Finally he removed her drawers completely. He pulled yet another extension of the odd bench she leaned against from underneath, forcing her knees apart. This made it impossible to close her thighs.

He stepped over to the wall to choose his weapon. She watched as he stroked his long fingers down each of his whips, lingering on the different tips. Katrina's breath came forth in short pants.

In her opinion, he'd dallied before his collection entirely too long. "Hurry," she murmured.

"Patience, my impish girl."

Her body began to shake, which puzzled her because the room's temperature was comfortable. She returned her attention to Maxwell and observed him take the first whip she'd noticed off the wall—the one with the wide, soft leather end.

He stood behind her for a few moments then she heard the rustling of fabric. Turning her head, she saw that he was in the process of removing his waistcoat, neck cloth and dress shirt.

Good God. What had she got herself into?

Finally he stood at her backside, pressing against her so that she could feel the hard length of his erection bearing down on her naked bum cheeks and the heat of his bare chest as he leaned over her. She watched as he brought the whip around to the front of her. Taking an end in each hand, he pressed it gently just beneath her breasts. He then drew it up over her nipples and back down again, over and over.

"I've got you in my trap and now I'll never let you go," Maxwell whispered.

Katrina closed her eyes, letting the sensation wash over her, allowing the gooseflesh to titillate her senses. A tiny moan escaped her as she tilted her head back.

"Your body is so reactive, my little mouse."

She should protest the use of that silly nickname he'd given her. But then decided that he could call her whatever he wished as long as he pleasured her in this wanton manner.

She felt something softly draw tiny circles down her spine. "That first time you left me on Lovat Lane I wanted to find you and have at your sweet cheeks with such a heated vengeance…"

He'd spoken so quietly she had to strain to listen.

"I wanted to strip you naked and tie you to a rack in some dungeon."

Katrina's breath caught. He painted the naughtiest pictures in her mind.

"Perhaps I'd let the other guards watch me whip your silky arse then take you from behind."

Before she could react, Maxwell took the whip and nudged a curtain aside upon the wall before her, a bit higher than eye level. An angled mirror hung there. He stepped away from her and moments later, the mirror revealed another reflection as a second set of curtains was pushed aside on the opposite wall. She gazed into it and realized it was Maxwell's naked back she saw, and her bottom, bared to him — entirely at his mercy.

He caressed her skin just before the first blow landed.

She went rigid, but, surprisingly, it didn't hurt as much as she'd thought it would. Another landed, more intense than the first. Then a third hit — the hardest of the three. She hissed an intake of breath.

"Mm. It seems we've found the beginning of your pain threshold. Let's see how far we can push you."

Five fierce blows in a row smacked against her bum. Her skin throbbed severely, but it felt oh, so good. Would he go further? He couldn't possibly be finished, could he? It wasn't enough. No, not by a long run.

Maxwell dragged the soft tip of the whip over the welts on her bottom. "More?"

Refusing to beg aloud, she didn't reply, but hoped to heaven he'd continue.

Seven, harsher blows cracked against her tingling cheeks, leaving Katrina shaken and needy. *Yes, oh, yes.*

"Now remain very still. I'm going to give you twenty strokes this time. If you don't cry out or move, I shall reward you most pleasurably."

Katrina fisted the restraints in her hands, ready to take her punishment and earn his promised heaven. A trickle of sweat formed at her temple and threatened to slide down her cheek. She wanted desperately to scratch at it, but she sensed that within their titillating game, the penalty for her disobedience would be too great.

His twenty blows hit every inch of her exposed bottom that hadn't been touched before by the whip. She thought she'd never sit again, so intense was the sting.

Maxwell walked over to the wall of whips and Katrina, trying to catch her breath, rubbed her sweat-dampened face on her arm, quickly so as not to alert him.

"You did so very well, mouse," he said as he replaced his naughty device back upon the peg. He walked to the opposite wall. She watched him take down the feather fan and come once again to stand at her side. "Now be a good girl and come for me." Then his hand slipped around the front of her, and he slid his fingers between her thighs, working her clitoris in tiny circles.

Katrina moaned a luxurious, sensual sound.

With the feathers he fanned the burning flesh of her bottom, stroking it lightly over her skin, easing the sting. "My God, how creamy you are," he whispered. He eased two fingers inside her and out just as quickly, only to toy with her nubbin again. He stroked her in the same fashion that he'd slid those wicked beads of his in. Up and down, his digits strummed her instead of the jade. Katrina's arms ached, but she needed to orgasm so badly she ignored the pain.

"You want to come?"

"Yes," she breathed.

"You want to feel that sweet release, don't you? The building up, holding your breath until rapture overtakes you, until your control snaps." The fan fell to the floor and he stroked her faster.

"Yes," Katrina panted.

With his free hand he pushed his finger into her vagina from behind. Still diddling her clitoris from the front, he stroked the opening of her anus with his other thumb.

"I am so going to fuck you after you come," he whispered into her ear.

Nudged over the edge, she screamed as her orgasm hit. He sank his fingers deep inside her, lifting her up, her toes hardly touching the ground. "Yes, fuck my hands, that's it."

She pumped her hips with short, jerking motions while she rode the blissful waves of electricity that pulsed all the way to her soul.

Maxwell finally released her. He unwrapped her wrists and she leaned upon the bench, shaking as echoes of delight thrummed through her body. She barely noticed when he slid the underside of the bench back into place and was vaguely aware that he'd removed the rest of his clothes.

He came up behind her and separated her bum cheeks, tilting her hips forward. "I'm sorry," he murmured, "but I have to have you. Right now."

His cock penetrated the lips of her slick vagina and without mercy, he drove into her.

"God, your arse is so hot from my whip."

Katrina held onto the bench while her tender bottom bounced against his hips and thighs. Glorious orgasms that reached from her toes to her skull rippled through her, both of them singing their pleasure. It was almost deafening in the small room.

The final ten or so powerful thrusts before he came nearly shattered Katrina. Maxwell held her gently by the hips. "Don't move," he panted. "God. I've never come so hard." Moments later, he disengaged from her, but not without his breath catching as he did so. He led her over to the couch-sized bench, and they sprawled across it, limbs slick with sweat, heavy and entwined.

Chapter Eighteen

Max eyed Katrina over his eggs and sausage. She'd barely uttered five words to him since he'd whipped her last night. And now, hindsight nagged at him from the shadowy corners of his mind, plaguing him about his ill treatment of her. He should have offered to talk about what they'd done in his playroom after he'd taken her back to reality—back into his bed. They'd fallen asleep so quickly that conversation had been inadvertently sidestepped.

He took a sip of his tea, using the motion as an excuse to glance up at her. Hell, it seemed she couldn't even look at him today. Whatever was on her plate had captured her interest entirely. He set the cup gingerly upon its saucer and dabbed at the corners of his mouth with his linen napkin. Had she hated being tied up and swatted with a buggy whip? Had she enjoyed the sex afterwards? He'd taken her quite brutally from behind, after all—even before he'd had the chance to ease the pain of her welted skin. Did she despise him for his sexual depravities?

"I beg your pardon, sir." Simmons came into the room and broke up the boxing match Max was losing with his conscience. "Here is this morning's copy of *The Times*."

"Thank you, Simmons." His butler handed him the newspaper. "Don't think they've ever been this late."

"Indeed." Simmons departed from the breakfast room leaving Max once again alone with Katrina. "Um—"

She glanced up at him, seemingly for the first time since leaving his room early this morning, her expression expectant.

"Would you be interested in reading the paper?"

"Oh, no, thank you." She refocused on cutting her sausage into bite-sized pieces.

Max stifled a harrumph. Was that all the conversation he'd get from her today? He slumped against the chair back and snapped open the paper, frustrated with himself for his deficient interaction.

He sat up at first sight of one of the lesser headlines. "Dash it. I'd almost forgotten."

"What is it?"

"They published Charles' dissertation. This is the day he's been waiting for." He reached over and rang a silver bell. "Good God, we'd forgotten about this before we made our plans to meet at his office about Brenner. I'll need to get to him at home before anyone else calls this morning. We'll need a plan B, now that he'll be the talk of the *ton* and in the spotlight of every gossip within a twenty mile radius."

"May I—"

Simmons re-entered the room and Max stood. "Have the landau brought 'round as soon as possible."

"Yes, sir. I'll tell Cook she can have it for the shopping upon your return."

"Excellent," Max said as Simmons departed.

Katrina eased her chair back by herself. "Maxwell, may I come with—"

"No!" He hadn't meant to answer so quickly and with such vigor. "It's... It's just that last night I saw two of Brenner's thugs walking down Hamilton Place, which means they aren't only sticking to the rougher areas of town."

She remained seated. "Oh. I see."

He felt like a complete cad.

"May I at least go outside for some air? I—I promise to stay behind the walls. I'd like to see the garden and stable...in the daylight."

"Of course. I didn't mean to—"

"It's all right." She stood and placed her napkin next to her plate. "I know you didn't mean it." She started to walk around the table.

Maxwell Aurelius Courtland, say something, you idiot! "Um—"

Katrina paused at the doorway and looked at him. "Yes?"

"I—I should be back in time for luncheon."

Her brows rose above her exotic cat-like eyes, but she didn't utter a sound.

Max swallowed. "Perhaps we could...talk, then?"

She nodded. "Mmm." And left the room.

He could have dove in front of a hastily moving hackney right about now. He couldn't stand to leave her like this, and yet he had to go to Charles, if only for an hour or so. What he wouldn't have given for the ability to be in two places at once.

* * * *

During her soak in Maxwell's bathtub, Katrina pondered the reasons why Max had been so quiet at breakfast. Had she done something wrong in his hidden room? Should she have played more the helpless victim instead of taking his blows and liking it so much? He'd enjoyed taking his pleasure, that much he'd admitted aloud, but the rest... His lack of interaction this morning *had* to be connected to her behavior last night. There was no other explanation.

Now, out in the daylight, she paced back and forth just outside the French doors, within the walls of Maxwell's town home. The whole situation rolled around in her stomach resulting in an acute embarrassment. He'd never been at a loss for words since she'd known him. Why had he gone silent now? Surely it had something to do with her.

Katrina tried to shake the feeling off with a turn around the garden, not five paces from where she'd worn her own worry path on the lawn.

The herbs were kept separate from the non-edible flora by a narrow cobblestone path that also circled the quaint space. Birds twittered about, swooping in, out and around. The bees worked diligently at pollinating the blossoms. She sighed. Spring certainly had a curious effect on everything.

A horse whinnied in the stable next to the garden, drawing her attention across the yard to the buggy repair port. Other horse-like sounds emitted from the same direction. Strange, but they sounded happy. *How pitiful that a horse could seem in better spirits than me.* She exited the garden and crossed the wide strip of pavement. The lame conveyance was yet inside. However, the wheels had been attached since she'd hidden in the shadows the night of Maxwell's ball. She stepped inside and ran her hand down the cab's black lacquer. No windows yet, but it was coming along nicely. God, it seemed like weeks ago she had been here trying to relieve that woman of her diamonds. Reaching up, she opened the door to the carriage, remembering the two clandestine lovers and how they'd had a terrible time of it.

Odd, but Maxwell never seemed to have an awkward moment when they were in each other's arms. No, he was smooth like a well-aged cognac — and just as potent. Perhaps she'd let him take her out here, on the bench of this nearly restored carriage. Heat washed over her face and neck. She shut the door, but steadied herself on the window sill. Drawing in a breath of cooling air, she shut her eyes and tilted her head back. *What have I become?*

* * * *

Thank God Max had arrived at Charles and Susanna's when he did. Two minutes after he'd stepped into the parlor to discuss Brenner, droves of men and women callers began to pour in to congratulate him on his insightful article.

Unable to catch Charles alone, Max had stayed and helped Susanna receive her guests. He'd even played butler, ordering up pot after pot of tea while his sister and brother-in-law gracefully accepted sincere accolades from adoring friends and neighbors. All the while he felt as if he were about to explode. It was imperative that he and Charles have their discussion — strike at Brenner while the poker was hot, so to speak. In less than twenty-four hours, Brenner's suspicions, the ones that Max had noticed that the thief had held in check the last time they'd spoken, would prove disadvantageous and he'd probably skip town. Then they'd have no way of cornering him.

"Max, didn't you see me trying to signal you over?"

"Sorry? I was pouring tea for Susanna and—"

"Never mind." Charles took the china pot from Max, set it upon the tray and dragged him over to a corner of the parlor. "Listen. My friend Jonathan, who works for the Yard, was just here. I told him how to get to that *Den* you spoke of. Tonight, he and half of Scotland Yard are going to lead a raid and bring Brenner in. Therefore, neither you nor I need be in attendance."

"Brilliant. Your presence at said event was exactly what I wanted to avoid, now that everyone will be watching every move you make, owing to this morning's publicity."

"Yes, well, now you don't have to go, either." Charles blew out a breath. "I'll draft the appropriate papers so that the timing coincides. If we're lucky, they won't let that bastard Brenner out of jail before the trial."

Max knew Katrina would be apprehensive about the raid, but he'd do his best to assure her that all would be well. Perhaps he'd buy her some scented bath oils—he knew how much she enjoyed her baths. Such a gift would surely take her mind off her troubles.

* * * *

Max's carriage pulled up to the front of his town house and he alighted without the help of his driver. "Stay put, Martin. You're to take Cook shopping, I believe." Then Max took the stairs to his door two at a time, excited to see Katrina.

Once inside, Simmons greeted Max.

"Where is Miss Harwood?"
"Out back, taking the air, sir."

* * * *

Across the pavement and beyond the garden, the same horse nickered from inside the stable as it had just minutes ago. "There now. Settle down, lass," came a lilting Irish-accented voice from inside the shelter.

Katrina cocked her head to the side, ignoring all other noises but the utterance, and she froze. "That sounded like—no, it couldn't be." Her mind was playing tricks on her.

Still, she had to be certain. Picking up her skirts she then rushed through the door where Maxwell's horses were kept. At the sight of the new groom, Katrina lost the breath from her lungs.

"Have you seen a ghost, then?" Jimmy grinned and tossed the horse brush to the floor. The horse he'd been brushing swished its tail and stepped forward to investigate the contents of his trough.

She flew into Jimmy's embrace, hugging him fiercely, running her hands across his shoulders, up and down his arms and finally landing on either side of his face. "My God. I thought you were dead!" she sobbed. Utterly elated, she pulled his head toward hers, planting a kiss smack upon his parted lips.

He pulled her closer still, at first only letting her kiss him. Then he began to participate and in moments, he took over, running his hands up and down her back, kissing her as if they were lovers.

After allowing him to return her greeting, Katrina realized her mistake and, to avoid being rude—for it *was* she who had initiated the kiss, started to speak to him. "Susanna, that is, Lady Kendrick, said you'd been brutally beaten and stabbed. What happened?"

Jimmy wouldn't release her. "Oh, they did pummel me a bit, and it's likely I'll have a nasty scar from Brenner's knife, but I recovered just fine, as you can see." He bent his head to hers and kissed her cheeks. "Did you miss me, *cousin*?"

"Of course I did. I even went so far as to search for your body in a morgue."

"Me darlin' little heroine." He kissed her again on the mouth.

Katrina gently pushed at his shoulders and, after a noticeable effort, he finally permitted a draft of air between their bodies. "That will be quite enough," she whispered.

"Never enough. You're the only joy I've known in the last week." And he buried his face into the crook between her shoulder and ear.

"Come now. Tell me exactly what happened." She attempted to wiggle out of his arms but to no avail.

"Only if you quit your squirmin' an' be still."

Katrina huffed out a sigh. "Very well. *Talk*."

Jimmy pulled her over to a bale of hay and sat, taking her down onto his lap. "After Brenner tried to gut me, Artie and Oliver apparently tossed me into the Thames. I woke up in a shack. Some woman had bound my wound and nursed me. A few days later, the two brutes came around, stirring things up. So I figured I'd better get out before they found me."

"Good heavens. So how did you end up here?"

He shrugged a shoulder. "I was havin' a pint in the darkest corner of some shoddy pub when I heard a job had opened up at a fine town house on Hamilton Place. I came straight away and talked to some bloke named Simmons."

"So you lied to him?"

"Lied? Me?"

"Well surely you've never worked with horses before."

"Beggin' yer pardon, Miss Katrina, but groom was one of my first legit jobs as a young lad. As I said before, I wasn't always a pilfering scamp."

She laughed. "I'm so very happy you're all right, Jimmy. And your wound—you didn't contract a fever?"

"I did, indeed. It didn't last long, though. And as luck would have it, the gash hasn't done any bleedin' since yesterday." Jimmy lifted his shirt up and over his head and tossed it to the ground. "See? Me bandages are yet clean."

Katrina gingerly ran her hand across the white linen binding that covered his lower abdomen when, from the door to the stable, someone cleared his throat.

Chapter Nineteen

Max watched Katrina's mouth open and close while in the arms of her lover like a carp out of water. He'd not paid any notice when Brenner had made the observation that Katrina and the boy had been 'chummy'.

"Maxwell." She leaped from Jimmy's lap. The boy grabbed up his shirt and hastily shrugged into it. "This is my friend Jimmy—the man we thought had been killed."

"We've met," Max said sharply, hiding his surprise.

"Yes—and now I gotta get back to these horses."

"Just a moment." Regardless of his rioting emotions, Max knew Charles could use Jimmy's cooperation to bring down Brenner. "There's going to be a raid on the Den tonight and I'd like your help, Jimmy."

Katrina jumped into the conversation. "Oh, but, Maxwell, he can't possibly go—"

"I'm not asking him to go back," he said without looking at Katrina. "My brother-in-law is going to be the prosecuting attorney and we'd be most grateful if you would testify against Brenner."

Jimmy eyed Max. "And will I be implicated in the process as well?"

"No. Quite the opposite. In fact, I am convinced you'll get a full pardon for your participation."

"If you could guarantee that—"

"I will. So do we have an agreement?"

Jimmy glanced at Katrina who nodded her encouragement. "All right, I'll do it."

"Great. I'll get a message to Charles." Max turned to go.

"Might I stay on here then?"

Max smiled but wasn't concerned whether it looked sincere or not. Katrina's young paramour was back from the dead, and Max had lost the only woman he had ever loved. "Of course you can." He quit the stables and strode for the house.

"Wait, Maxwell."

He didn't heed the feminine request but increased his pace.

"Stop, Maxwell. Please."

Max sighed and paused on the path.

"In spite of what that might have looked like, it's not what you think."

Without looking at her, he replied, "You have no idea what I think, Miss Harwood."

* * * *

It was nearly breakfast time and Katrina's throat was raw from crying. She couldn't get Maxwell to listen to her no matter what approach she took, and it plagued her like the Devil. Last night, after she had heard him retire, she'd slipped a note under his door, but within minutes it had been shoved back under the door to her room, unopened. Yesterday he'd told her she had no idea what he was thinking, and that was the rub. If she knew what was going through his mind—however wrong he was, she was confident that she could convince him otherwise—convince him that she was not in love with Jimmy, but with *him*. All she needed from him was an admittance of his suspicions and she could clear things up with one sentence.

She leaned her head on the mantelpiece. *Maxwell.*

A knock came at the door. "Yes?" Katrina croaked, her voice sounding just like a bullfrog.

"It's me, Mrs Dillard."

She cleared her throat the best she could. "Come in."

The woman brought in a tray Katrina was determined to once again refuse. "I—"

"No you don't. I let you turn away the last two meals and Mr Simmons will have my head if this one comes back untouched." She placed the food upon a small table between the fireplace and a comfortable blue brocade-covered chair.

Katrina sighed in surrender. "All right. But I'm not hungry."

"Be that as it may, you'll have to eat or I'll be sacked."

Knowing very well Simmons wouldn't sack Mrs Dillard, Katrina sat down and Mrs Dillard pushed the table close to her.

She'd have to admit, the hot tea soothed her throat, but her stomach felt too occupied with apprehension about Maxwell. "Mrs Dillard, have you seen Mr Courtland yet today?"

"I did. He ate early and went directly to his study."

Katrina set her tea cup down and inched closer to the edge of her chair. The downstairs rooms were connected by arches and doorways. Perhaps if she took the book she'd borrowed to read back to the library, she could inadvertently wander into the study. Then Maxwell would *have* to listen to her!

Pretending to be occupied with stirring her tea, she asked, "And... He's there *now*?"

Mrs Dillard folded her arms over her chest. "I'll answer that when half of your plate is clean."

This is what it must be like to have a gaoler. Determined to get her answer, Katrina carelessly shoveled the scrambled eggs into her mouth — not paying any mind that she'd used her tea spoon to do so. She practically swallowed one of the sausages whole, and by the second potato, Mrs Dillard gained her attention.

"Careful now, or it'll come right back up."

"Half. You said half!" A piece of food went flying out of her mouth, but she didn't care.

"Och. Chew that and swallow it properly." She handed Katrina a napkin. "I don't need to see the contents of your mouth while ya eat."

Katrina took the napkin, unfolded it with a shake and wiped her mouth. "There, see? Half."

"Open that napkin, young lady." Mrs Dillard pointed to the linen in her hands.

"What, do you think I'd spit my food out?"

"Just open it. We'll discuss it when I see what you've done."

Katrina hesitated, thankful that she'd decided to swallow her food instead of leaving the chewed contents of her mouth tucked inside the linen. She reached out her hand and opened the napkin. "See?"

Her smug tone didn't move Mrs Dillard in the least. "I've had three sons. They're grown now, but I know all the tricks."

"So is Mr Courtland in his study or not?"

Mrs Dillard smiled as if she'd gotten her way. "Last I looked, he was."

Katrina nearly overturned the tray as she ran to her bedside to grab her book. Mrs Dillard caught the edge just in time.

"Thank you, Mrs Dillard. You're a dear!"

Mrs Dillard railed at her, but Katrina couldn't hear the words as she was in the midst of dashing downstairs to find Maxwell. She'd clear up this misunderstanding if she had to follow him all the way to the necessary.

Katrina knew exactly which shelf she'd originally pulled the sentimental volume from. In fact, she could see the empty spot from across the room. But she needed to kill some time in order to peek into the study—*entirely* by mistake, of course. She'd feign surprise—maybe even drop her book, startled by his presence.

She slid her finger along the 'A' authors, mumbled along the 'B' and 'C' authors as if reading the names— the 'D and E' authors went by in a blur, until she stood one bookcase away from the entrance to Maxwell's study.

Here we go.

She took a deep breath and crossed the path that led to the study.

Her book fell to the floor—toward the study. "Oops!" She stepped through the doorway and picked up the book.

But Maxwell wasn't there. Simmons was, and in the process of filling the desk lamp with oil.

"Oh. Simmons."

He paused. "Miss Harwood. Can I help you?"

"I—I was looking for Mr Courtland."

"Mr Courtland has gone to run some errands. Anything I can do?"

"No, no. I was just...putting this book away." She turned back to the library and shoved the book back into place.

Shite.

Even if she decided to pick up another book, it wouldn't do any good. She couldn't concentrate on reading a street sign right now. Turning on her heel, she stormed out and up the stairs to wait out the day in her room.

Mrs Dillard was still there, making the bed. "So, did you see him?"

"No," she said, deflated. "He's gone out." She sat back down in the blue chair, the remains of her cold, unfinished breakfast mocking her pain from the tray.

"If it's any solace, I know for a fact that he's expecting you for supper."

"How do you know that?"

"I heard him tell Simmons to make sure he had a place set for you for tonight."

Well, I suppose that's some sort of step toward an actual conversation with Maxwell. "Thank you, Mrs Dillard."

* * * *

The staff were in the process of clearing Maxwell's dessert plate as she entered the dining room at five minutes to eight. His seat was vacant.

This was beginning to get ridiculous. She turned to find Simmons when he entered. "Ah, Simmons. Where is Mr Courtland?"

"Mr Courtland has gone to see Lord and Lady Kendrick."

"Thank you." She made to exit the room when he stopped her.

"Please, Miss Harwood. Sit and have something to eat. You've hardly partaken of anything in the last two days. Is it the cooking?"

She owed Simmons some sort of explanation. "No, of course not. I guess I'm just in a nervous state, is all."

His shoulders seemed to relax a bit. "It must be going around." He indicated the open newspaper next to Max's place. "That is the same excuse Mr Courtland gave just before he left this evening. Will that be all, Miss Harwood?"

Katrina's gaze fell upon the headline, *'Thief Ring Exposed, Linchpin Taken Into Custody'*. She took up the paper to read the article. "No, Simmons, thank you."

Barely able to breathe, she fell into Max's chair and absorbed every word. The article noted that Scotland Yard had raided 'a nest of thievery' and a man named Larson Brenner had been brought in. All sorts of charges had been named, and many items had been confiscated from the warehouse where the raid had taken place. The Yard asked anyone who had been robbed within the last two months to come forward, and if their description matched any of the evidence procured, they would be allowed to press additional charges.

This could very well be the end of Brenner, if things went right. Odd, but the article didn't mention whether any of the others had been brought in. Did they know Brenner had been taken in? Had Scotland Yard placed officers near the Den in order to bring in the rest of the thieves at a later time?

No, this wouldn't do at all. Some of those men were there because they had nowhere else to go—just as she'd had nowhere else to go after her father died. If Maxwell hadn't come along when he had, that could very well have been her about to be pounced on by the authorities.

Something needed to be done—someone had to go and warn the rest of them—*tonight*.

Chapter Twenty

Having donned her mourning gown, Katrina slipped out of the front door. The evening air was cold. She wondered at the fact that after only a few days with access to a warm, comfortable bed, she wasn't used to the gnawing dampness of a night on the streets.

Despite her circumstances, she knew it wouldn't have been prudent to depart for the Den from the back of the house, because Jimmy was sure to try to talk her out of the scheme. He'd likely insist on tagging along, but who knew what would befall him this time if he confronted the thieves—*if* there were any that had lingered after the raid.

Alternatively, her former associates might have all scattered once they found out that Brenner was gone. Endless scenarios progressed through her mind as if she were reading them aloud from a list. Whatever the reason turned out to be, Katrina had to make sure the place was abandoned. Her conscience demanded that she do so.

She'd kept to the waterfront for a good mile or more, looking behind her every now and again as to be positive she hadn't been followed. Discovering one of the ways that led to an entrance to the Den, she tiptoed inside and made her way through the labyrinth of corridors until she reached the inner sanctum. It seemed deserted—dark. Not even a glimmer of light. They must have gotten the hint and scattered. She peered up at the catwalks that led to the rooms above, when she was seized by the arm. A scream rose up in her throat, but bitter fear hindered its release.

"What the 'ell are you doin' 'ere?"

"I—I—" She gasped for air. "You scared the Devil out of me, Oliver."

"I asked you a question."

The flame of a match flared, ignited a candle wick, and in the small circle of light Katrina saw about a dozen familiar faces.

"Returnin' to the scene of the crime, I'll wager," one of the men accused.

"Not at all. I've come to—"

"What I want to know is, what did she have to do with last night's raid?" another one asked.

"I beg your pardon," Katrina said with no small amount of indignation "I came because I read in the paper that Mr Brenner had run into some trouble."

Oliver scoffed. "Heh, 'run into some trouble.' That's a fine way of puttin' it."

"She's guilty, no doubt," one of them announced, rolling up his sleeves as if he had a dirty job to do.

"Those blokes took it all. Cleaned us out. Even Brenner's stash."

"An' it's all 'er fault!" a man shouted and pointed an accusing finger in her face.

Katrina blinked at the action.

"What to do wif 'er is the next question."

"Do away wif 'er. She knows too much already."

They were firing statements at her so quick she couldn't figure out who'd spoken. "Now, gentlemen. You must understand—"

"We understand that you've always been able to waltz in and out of here by yer own will since you come to the Den." Oliver bared his yellow and black teeth at her.

"I smell a rat."

A tall, dirty ginger Scot, who normally kept to himself, stepped forward. "Or a pigeon."

"Just a moment. I won't be spoken to in this manner. I came here tonight to make sure the rest of you leave."

"Leave? What for?"

"Get yourselves out of town. What if they make Mr Brenner name names?"

"'E'd never do such."

"You don't know that! For heaven's sake, listen to reason!"

"She has a point, but I still don't believe she's innocent of turnin' Brenner in," the Scot scoffed, spun on his heel and stalked away from the circle.

Oliver agreed with a nod. "An' if she didn't turn 'im in, then it's that Jimmy Lock. He wanted out anyway, recall it?"

Every one of their faces turned to her and her entire body went numb. "D-don't be ridiculous. Jimmy is dead."

"Is 'e now?"

"I don't fink 'is body was ever found."

She swallowed, hoping no one noticed. "What does that prove? Perhaps he was...eaten...by dogs or something."

A stirring of murmured doubt echoed through the filthy lot and she took advantage of it. "Look, all of you, I'm telling the truth. I came here tonight to make sure whoever was left got out of town before anything else happens."

Oliver finally let her go and chimed in. "This is gettin' us nowheres. We'd 'a' known by now if she was followed, and besides that, 'er daft suspicions have managed to crawl under my skin. I'm gonna take 'er advice and leave. It's safer than stickin' 'round 'ere, anyway."

One of the other men took Katrina by the arm. "If I find out that bloody *Lock* had anything to do with this, I'll 'unt both of you down and feed you to the dogs meself."

His grip loosened slightly and she pulled away. "There will be no need for that, I'm sure." She smoothed her damp hands down the front of her dress.

"I'll take 'er outside. The rest of you break it up." Oliver took hold of her once again and escorted her through an entirely different way than she'd ever taken before. It confused her something dreadful and she suddenly didn't know north from south. An impulsive dread washed over her, threatening to drown her. Luckily, they ended up in a familiar spot and she relaxed some. Beyond the next corridor and to the right lay Lovat Lane.

"Just so's you know, I too will be on the lookout for Mr Lock. An' even if I find out 'e didn't have nuffin' to do with the raid, I'll dispose of him—*properly* dis time."

"I understand," she said without flinching. He released her and she made her way out, quite hastily, to Lovat Lane.

Katrina hurried along the deserted street, trying to silence the shuffle of her footsteps by walking on the balls of her feet, when a noise sounded behind her. She paused, straining to repeat it in her mind to possibly determine the origin. It had been something between a crackle and the scuff of a shoe. Footsteps— *human* footsteps. For heaven's sake, she was almost to the end of Lovat Lane. They couldn't, *wouldn't* have followed her. She'd gone to save them—she'd said her peace and left. Honor demanded that they let her go without incident.

Honor. Thieves had no honor. And without Jimmy and, ironically, without Brenner, Katrina was at the mercy of who was left of the East Side Den of Thieves.

Katrina hiked up her skirts and broke into a run. With terror at her heels and a scream lodged in her throat, her heart strained to pump blood and send energy to her laboring muscles.

Even above her own heavy breathing, there it was— the sound of pounding, hasty footsteps coming from behind. Exactly which thief hunted her, she couldn't say.

She rounded the first corner, lamenting that she'd long passed the maze of alleyways that had in the past hidden her so well. She had to make it to a populated area—a place where there were dozens of people milling about—then perhaps her pursuer would cry off and leave her be.

But hell if she could find one.

Good God. Has everyone gone to bed? It's bloody early yet!

Suddenly she was seized from behind, plucked off the ground. She struggled to draw enough air into her lungs to unleash the Devil's own scream when her captor spoke.

"Goddamn it, Katrina. What the hell do you think you're doing out here?"

It was Maxwell.

Pins prickled her every nerve ending as she swallowed her shout for help.

"Put me down! Heavens, you scared the shite out of me!"

"*I* frightened you?" He set her upon the ground and spun her around to face him, hauling her against his body. "You came down here, all alone, placed yourself in that hive and *I* frightened you? Christ, they could have killed you. Or worse!"

"I'm fine, as you can see," she murmured, her heart still hammering in her ears. She glanced in the direction of the Den. "Though it would be prudent not to linger. So if you don't mind, release me and we can get out of here."

"Oh, now, here's a lane we've traveled down before," he mocked sardonically. "I'm not letting you go. You'll run." He turned, pulling her with him, and strode down the street. "We'll talk when we get home."

She had to hasten her steps just to keep up with him. "So all I have to do is run away to get you to sit down for a decent conversation with me?"

Maxwell stopped and maneuvered her so that she stood in front of him. He glared down at her. "And just what is that supposed to mean?"

"It means I've been trying to talk to you and you've succeeded in avoiding me in such an exacting way that I may as well have been pursuing a ghost. I don't like being ignored, Maxwell, especially when I have something important to say."

He shoved her aside without letting go and continued on his path, eating up yards with his long strides. "I don't need to hear your excuses as to why I found you in the arms of another man—"

"Jimmy is not another man. He's—"

"Someone whom you care deeply for. You admitted it yourself."

"Ooo, you are impossible!" How could she convince him otherwise? They rounded a corner and Maxwell's landau came into view. "Look. It's not what you think. This whole thing is—"

"Not up for debate. Seeing is believing, and I saw you kissing each other. *Passionately.* It wasn't a simple greeting, nor was it a peck on the cheek. It was your body pressed to his—your closed eyes. I even heard you murmuring softly to each other—words of love, perhaps?"

Unable to produce a verbal defense, her strangled protest came out in an ineffective squeak.

"You may as well confess. You were so lost in his kisses that you didn't even hear me enter the stables."

As angry as he was—which couldn't possibly suppress the equivalent of her swiftly mounting fury—he hoisted her into the cab. "If you run now, it will only serve as an admission to your guilt." She watched with a burning anger in her stomach as he slammed the door behind her, climbed into the driver's seat and took up the reins.

The carriage lurched forward, and while they sped down the side streets of London, she railed at him. "You don't understand! I was merely glad he wasn't dead!" Maxwell didn't respond. "You idiot! You sit in judgment from that high throne of yours and you have no idea what's really going on! And I thought you so damned smart."

After a few moments, she realized that the glass window between the cab and the driver's seat was preventing her from being heard. If there was one thing in this world that made her as mad as a wet hornet, it was when someone refused to communicate. Her bloody father used to do that to her when she needed to voice her opinion. Well, hell if she was going to sit there and do nothing. She reached up, detached the leather strap that held the transparent barrier in place, lowered it down and watched it disappear into the slot between the seats. Cold air rushed into the cab, but she didn't care. Katrina climbed over the window opening, her skirts shoving up to her waist, blowing in the wind, and she slid into the seat next to Maxwell.

He glanced at her, his full lips pursed in annoyance.

"Stop this carriage at once, Maxwell! We need to hash this out before we get to Hamilton Place!"

"And why is that?"

"Because I won't have you screaming at me in front of the staff." It was a stupid excuse, but she figured she needed to appeal to his sensibilities somehow.

Maxwell was considering her request, she could sense it.

Finally, resignation showed on his face and he pulled the horses to a stop. Had they been there during the day, the shops would have been filled with people, but at this late hour, they were closed for the night.

At once he took her into his arms and kissed her, his mouth brutally devouring hers. She let him kiss her, participating occasionally when the pressure of his lips would let up. However, just as quickly, he drew her forward again, silently demanding her submission. He slid one of his hands from her waist to caress the outside of her thigh, her hip, her bottom—his palm heating the cotton of her drawers, threatening to ignite the fabric.

When he tangled his fingers in the bow that held the undergarment in place, Katrina moaned her encouragement. Frantic with the want of him, she tore her lips from his. "Yes, take me, Maxwell. I want you. Only you."

In the process of tugging at the tie, he stilled. "No." And he released her.

"Maxwell. Don't do this." She pressed her body to his side and tried to loop her arms around his neck. "Please…" When he didn't react, her voice trailed off.

"I'm not going to give you what you want. I'm going to punish you."

Her breath caught in her throat.

"Not that kind of punishment," he murmured bitterly. "In my present impassioned state I wouldn't be able to control myself and your bottom would be blistered for real."

Katrina opened her mouth, but again, when confronted with having to defend her own honor, she couldn't find the words.

"No. I'll take you home and you can visit your lover for your needs." He retrieved the reins and snapped the horses into a trot.

Through her tears, the rest of the ride home was a blur.

Chapter Twenty-One

The four weeks leading up to Brenner's trial were lonesome ones. Maxwell had successfully avoided Katrina and Katrina didn't dare seek out Jimmy's company. She felt as if she were stranded on a deserted island. She'd read nearly ever damned book in Maxwell's library that remotely interested her but was lonelier than she'd ever been in her life. The only persons she conversed with were Mrs Dillard and Simmons, but day-to-day business didn't produce the same effect in her heart as friendly companionship would have.

Early on, she'd received a note from Susanna. Because Katrina hadn't been called as a witness, there was no need for her to attend the trial. She was told not to worry about Susanna, as Charles had arranged it so that she could give her testimony directly to the judge and in front of the attorneys while remaining anonymous to the public. Whereas this information removed a significant load off Katrina's shoulders, Maxwell yet avoided her, which fed her psyche a different class of torment.

In fact, he hadn't appeared at any of the meals served in his own dining room since the hearing had started five days ago.

Even the way she kept up on the progression of Brenner's trial felt as if she were set apart from society. Her host, slyer than the Devil himself, had one of the staff cut articles from various newspapers and have them delivered to her wherever she was the moment they arrived at the house. It frustrated her beyond measure that Maxwell wouldn't even hold a relevant conversation with her.

She had no idea what he had planned for her once the trial was over. Would he immediately have her thrown onto the street? Would he send her a note to have her things out in twenty-four hours? Would he give her any sort of recommendation at all? Her mind whirred with similar, endless torments that churned the contents of her stomach into bricks.

Then there was the matter of her heart. If she had the good fortune of actually finding a decent place to live, could she ever trust again or would the winter of her life arrive to find a lonely, bitter old spinster? Katrina felt her emotions on the verge of breaking once again. *Oh, Maxwell—*

"My goodness, it's dark in here," Susanna said as she entered. She threw open the draperies of the parlor, bringing Katrina out of her gloomy thoughts.

Katrina thrust aside her sorrow and held up her hand to shield her eyes from the late-afternoon sunlight. "Is it over?"

Susanna sat next to her on the settee and stripped off her gloves. "Indeed it is," she beamed. "We won. Your friend Mr Lock, that is, Mr Blaylock, the one I thought murdered, has been pardoned for his testimony. I was sure he'd be mobbed by all the women who swooned over him. And that awful Mr Brenner is going to be tossed into Newgate for twenty years. I think he should have gotten life, but Charles says the defense attorney was a clever chap."

"I'm so happy for you and Lord Kendrick, Susanna. It was a well-deserved victory, to be sure." Katrina's smile was sincere, regardless of the uncertainty of her immediate circumstances. "It must have been very exciting for you."

"Indeed. My very favorite part, aside from the reading of the sentence, was when that Madame Dubois testified. She's rather beautiful for a woman of her age."

"Who is Madame Dubois?"

Susanna leaned forward as if she were about to reveal a great secret. "Why, Madame Dubois owns a *bordello!*" she whispered. "Very scandalous."

"Odd that her name didn't make the papers."

"Let's just say she didn't make the *news*papers."

"Oh, I see. What did she say at the trial?"

"Apparently, just before his arrest, Mr Brenner had been *recovering* from a visit to Madame Dubois, where he was somehow able to acquire valuables from the place. Madame Dubois offered descriptions of the stolen items that just happened to have been taken from Mr Brenner's hideout."

"When you said 'recovering', what exactly did you mean?"

"*Well,*" Susanna was back to whispering again, "I've heard tell that at Madame Dubois', they practice all sorts of naughty things on their clientele."

This intrigued Katrina, remembering Maxwell's hidden room she'd probably never see again. "Like what, do you suppose?"

"Oh, heavens. Playing pony and capture and having spankings… You know, things one should only do in the privacy of one's own home. I've read about such places in my Marvels, but the written imagery didn't go into nearly as much detail as what I've heard on the street."

"On the street, as in…?"

"Well, not exactly 'the street' but from some of the ladies in my circle…and some from Charles." She'd added the latter so quickly, Katrina almost didn't hear it.

"Ah." Poor Susanna's cheeks were as red as strawberries. Katrina decided to change the subject before the dear girl ignited like a firework. "So, where are Maxwell and your husband at the moment?"

"Well, Charles was set upon by the papers the second he stepped onto the pavement, and Maxwell agreed to stay with him until the crush retreated. Mr Lock, or rather Mr Blaylock's hackney pulled 'round back just as I was jumping out of mine to come see you."

"Thank you, Susanna. Had it not been for your visit, I would have had to wait until the papers come out tomorrow to hear how it all turned out."

"Then it is as I suspected. You and Maxwell have had a tiff."

"A tiff is putting it lightly. How did you figure it out?"

"Simply that my brother hasn't spoken of you in what seems like weeks."

Katrina deflated some. "I'm afraid it's over, Susanna. Maxwell—"

"Nonsense. I don't believe that for a second."

"It's true. I'm not even sure if I'll be allowed to stay here now that the trial is over. I'm hoping at least he'll let me stay until I can find a suitable situation."

"You won't be going anywhere. I know my brother and you have nothing to fear. After he barks some — and, trust me on this, his bite is virtually non-existent. What happens next is that he gets very quiet. He retreats. He goes into hibernation, but eventually he'll warm back up."

Katrina didn't want to argue with her friend. "We'll see," was all she offered.

Susanna patted her on the knee. "Now go freshen up and put on that glorious smile of yours. Maxwell should be home soon and we will all be able to put the wretchedness of this trial behind us. I should like to have you and Maxwell 'round for supper on Friday." From somewhere in the house, a clock struck five. "Heavens, I must be going." She began to pull on her gloves.

"Can't you stay for some tea? How long has it been since you've eaten?"

"No, my dear. And don't worry about me. I have a few more visits to make before I head home and I'm sure to be plied with pre-supper refreshments until I can no longer move."

They stood and Susanna kissed Katrina's cheeks. "Ta, darling. And don't forget about Friday."

"I won't." And Maxwell's sister swept from the room.

If only she possessed the kind of optimism that Susanna had. Dare she even hope for a second that what her friend said was true? This not knowing for sure was almost as bad as accepting the inevitable, that Maxwell hated the very sight of her and would, upon his return home this very afternoon, thrust her from his sight.

This thought process was not only getting her nowhere, but made her feel helpless in every circumstance affiliated with her person.

Every circumstance save…

Recalling that Susanna had mentioned that Jimmy had arrived at Hamilton Place, Katrina shook off her shroud of pity and ventured out of the back door to find him.

Looming in the back of her mind since just after the raid on the Den had been the threats on Jimmy's life made by the remaining thieves. There were things that needed to be said that Katrina was sure Jimmy wasn't ready to hear, but God help her, she was going to say them if only for his welfare. At least in this situation she could be of assistance.

She found him inside the tack room, organizing some tools.

He looked up as she entered and smiled.

"I heard you were a sensation on the witness stand."

"They made me name names. What they failed to recognize is that no one ever used their given names at the Den."

"That's not what I meant. I meant your admirers." Katrina picked up a hammer and placed it in one of the piles of tools he'd laid out.

He waved a hand in dismissal. "What would I want from a bunch o' society women?" He dusted off a chisel with a rag and set it upon a shelf.

"Anything you could get, I'd imagine." She drew her fingers down the length of a few neatly stacked screwdrivers assembled in a small wooden box.

"No thanks. Besides, me heart belongs to someone else." He dusted off his hands and pulled her into an embrace. "Where've you been hidin', m'lady? I've missed you."

"Jimmy, listen to me."

"The only thing I want to do is kiss those lips o' yours."

She put her hands between them and pushed at his chest. "No. Now stop this nonsense. What I have to say is entirely serious."

He sighed and released her. "Go on, then."

"The night after the authorities raided the Den, I went there to scatter whoever was left."

"You went there alone? Are ya daft?"

Katrina held up her hand to stop his tirade. "Please. I've been reprimanded enough over my actions. The point is, they'll be looking for you—all of them—especially now that they know for sure you're still alive. They want retribution, and as you know, there are people in this world who can't go on unless someone takes the blame for the shortcomings of this life."

"I'll be fine. I've lived on the streets for this long, haven't I?"

"Jimmy. What do you think will happen now that everyone in England knows your face? Each person at that trial will be able to point you out by sight. And when Brenner gets out, what do you suppose will be the first thing he will do?"

Mercifully, Jimmy went quiet as his gaze dropped to the floor. Finally, she was getting through to him.

"I suppose he'll track me down and do me in proper-like this time."

Katrina pushed aside the sinister picture he'd painted in her mind. "We can't let that happen. You need to leave. Go far away, where none of them will ever find you."

"And where do you propose I go? France? Spain? Africa?"

"America," she blurted, not knowing from where the suggestion came. "Not even Brenner would spend the money to go after you there."

"You've a logical argument, but there's one thing missin'."

"What's that?"

"You. Come away with me. There's nothin' I couldn't do with you by my side."

He made to pull her into his arms again, but she stopped him. "Jimmy, I can't go with you."

"Why not?"

"Because I'm desperately in love with Maxwell." She'd spoken without thinking, but now that it was out, now that every defense she possessed had been stripped away, well... There it was. The truth. It should have astounded her, but like a guardian angel, it seemed to have existed from the beginning of time.

"You're givin' away your heart to someone who is utterly unworthy. And on top o' that, he can't love you like I can. I care for you, I'd fight for you. Has he, at any point, fought to win your heart?"

Jimmy's words stung. "Perhaps it is up to me to fight for *his*."

"In my humble opinion, darlin', if a man isn't man enough to go after what he desires, then he doesn't deserve the prize."

Katrina chuckled bitterly. "For one so young, you sure have a deep knowledge of human behavior." She fought back the tears that she'd promised herself for the last few weeks she wouldn't shed.

After a few quiet moments passed, Jimmy finally spoke, "Maybe I just have an old soul."

"Of that I am positive." She looked him in the eye. "You are like a brother to me, Jimmy." He jerked his chin to the side as if to dismiss her statement, but she ventured forth, "Are we in agreement then that you need to get out of England?"

His big brown gaze scanned her features as if memorizing them, then he nodded.

"Good. I will arrange to take you to purchase passage tomorrow morning."

Jimmy shrugged.

"I'm only doing this because I care about you, you know."

"I know," he said just above a whisper.

"We'll leave very early, so be ready to go at first light."

"I shall."

She had almost turned to go when he stopped her. "Katrina?"

"Yes?" She looked up.

His eyes sparkled with unshed tears, but whether they were happy or sad tears, she couldn't tell. "Thank you."

"Until tomorrow morning."

* * * *

Maxwell held his breath as Katrina passed him on her way to the house. She hadn't caught him eavesdropping, and thank God for that.

He felt like a fool. He'd refused to speak to her for weeks now. He'd busied himself with Charles and the trial as much as possible. When he was home, like some spoiled child he had stomped about, barked at the staff, hardly eaten a thing, and been generally unpleasant to be around. Hell, Charles had even pointed out his ghastly behavior at the beginning of the trial.

And all because he'd misunderstood her actions toward the boy, and refused to listen to her explanation.

Idiot.

She'd tried to tell him the young man meant nothing more than a family member to her the night he'd caught her leaving that den of thieves.

Hope welled in his chest. She'd not three minutes ago confessed that she still loved him. But had she said that just to keep the boy's affections at bay? Did she really love Max? What if he'd lost her because of his hard-headedness? What if—?

This train of thought was taking him on a one way trip to Bedlam.

He needed to mend this rift and he'd do it tonight.

Chapter Twenty-Two

"A quarter past eight," Max intoned to himself — being the only living soul in the room — and replaced his pocket watch. He'd dressed in his best formal clothes for tonight's supper, anticipating his reunion with Katrina. He repeatedly tapped his fingers on the table in a pinky-to-index-finger march that echoed off the walls.

"Where the hell is she?"

He'd given a note to Mrs Dilllard with the distinct instruction to hand the message directly to Katrina. But now, hours later, he hadn't been given a reply. And who could blame her for her silence? He'd played hooky from his guest and every meal for the last five weeks. He supposed he deserved to eat in solitude.

Simmons entered the room and Max was pulled from his thoughts.

"Sir, your meal is getting cold, and Cook fears that the chicken will dry out if she reheats it one more time."

"I'm sorry. Yes. Please serve the meat course."

It wouldn't have mattered if Cook had reheated his chicken seventeen times. He'd choked it down and hadn't tasted a thing.

When Simmons came to take his plate, Max stopped him. "Have you seen Miss Harwood at all this evening?"

"No, sir. Shall I fetch Mrs Dillard to you? I'm sure she knows Miss Harwood's whereabouts."

"Yes, please."

Simmons bowed and left the room.

Max stared at the vacant chair opposite him. The china she would have used tonight remained spotless. Her crystal water goblet hadn't even been filled. This was not how he wanted to spend the rest of his life — sitting across from an empty place setting where Katrina should have been.

With a tap, a note was set next to Max. He glanced up in hopes that it was Katrina, but it was only Mrs Dillard.

"It's for you, from herself."

"Why hasn't she come down? Didn't she get my note?"

"She did. I imagine this is your answer."

"What's so important that she needed to reply via written word? Couldn't she just have told you yes that she'd be down to supper or not?"

"From what I've heard, you haven't exactly been a proper host for the last few weeks. Perhaps she's merely emulating your example."

Max felt his shoulders droop. He deserved the reprimand. "I know, and I'd like to make it up to her if I can."

"Well, you're in for it tonight."

He glanced up at Mrs Dillard. "What do you mean?"

"This is one of several notes she's prepared. We've nearly run out of stationery."

"I suppose I've earned whatever she's got planned."

"Well, she's set you on a merry chase thus far, hasn't she?"

Max chuckled. "And sometimes I can't tell if I'm the cat or the mouse."

"If you are over your head in love, then possessing the flexibility to be both is the key. That's how the late Mr Dillard and I remained happy for all those years." She gave him a nod. "Goodnight, sir."

"Goodnight, Mrs Dillard," he dismissed her and unfolded the note.

Leave your cravat at the table and find the naughtiest book in your library.

That wasn't at all what he'd expected to read. He stood, tucked the note into his trouser pocket and untied his cravat. "My 'naughtiest book'..." He grinned. "*The Kama Sutra.*" *What is she up to?* Laying the white silk tie across the back of his chair, he headed for the library.

Max imagined her walking along the bookcases at a leisurely pace, and perusing the titles. He entered and was slightly disappointed that she wasn't waiting therein. He scanned the full to bursting shelves around the room. Finally, he saw the book he was looking for, pulled out an inch farther than the others. It was in fact his *Kama Sutra* volume. He removed it from the shelf and found several pieces of paper sticking out from between the pages. Utterly puzzled, he carefully opened the cover to the first bookmark.

It read: '*There*'. He glanced at the couple depicted in the drawing. The female knelt, her bottom in the air, and the male had his cock inserted into her vagina from behind. Just the way that Max had taken Katrina in the playroom all those weeks ago. He swallowed. He'd been so angry lately that he hadn't thought about making love to her. Now, seeing the illustration, his John Thomas twitched, reminding him who was boss. He shook his head and turned to the next bookmark.

'*Is*'.

He flipped to the next marker. '*A*'.

The following one read, '*Clue*'.

He turned the pages faster and read the subsequent notes. '*On. Each. Of. These. Pages. That. Will. Tell. You. Where. To. Go. Next*'. The final note read, '*Leave your shirtsleeves in the library.*'

So, she wanted him to study the images, did she? He examined each one meticulously, growing ever so much hungrier for Katrina with each page. And the funny thing was, Max knew that *she* knew exactly what she was doing to him. "The little minx."

Finally, when he could stand to view the erotic images no longer, he snapped the book shut and slumped into the nearest chair. What did each of those pictographs have in common? "Pussies, big hard pricks, naked men and women having at each other, ecstasy…" With the back of his hand he wiped a sheen of sweat from his forehead. He stood and began removing his shirt.

There were other items depicted in the drawings. Platters of fruit, pillows, curtains. He knew she wasn't in the dining room, so the fruit plates weren't the clue, and there were curtains over every window in the house… Was she in the playroom? No. None of the pages she'd chosen showed any sort of extra apparatus.

Pillows... *Of course!* She was in his room!

He threw his shirt onto the chair, determined to get to his room as fast as his legs could carry him. He ran across the foyer, up the stairs, down the hall...

The door was shut. He grinned. She was probably spread out on his bed, naked and waiting for him.

He gave a little knock.

No response.

He rapped again.

Nothing.

He tried the knob and found that the door was unlocked. Entering, he strode into an empty room. The only thing on the bed was another note. He swore. If she didn't turn up soon he vowed to manipulate his cock until he came then go find her. Reaching for the note, he noticed that the door to the bathroom was shut. He smiled. That was where she was. All wet and naked, her sweet pussy submerged, waiting for him to come in and soap her down, rinse off the lather and lick the water away.

Fuck he was hard. He nearly disregarded the note on the bed, but his curiosity got the better of him.

Take the rest of your clothes off and join me.

Yes! She was in the tub.

He stripped his remaining clothes off and opened the door so hard a waft of air tousled his hair.

But she wasn't inside the bathroom.

"You've got to be joking." He stepped toward the dry tub and saw his dressing gown folded and laying at the bottom with a note sticking out of the pocket. Reaching down, he plucked the paper from its resting place.

Come to where we first met.

He harrumphed. *The study.* "Why, so I can find another clue to where you *aren't*?" He threw the note at the corner of the room, not giving a damn where it landed.

Well, she is running out of rooms in which to hide... Perhaps she'll be there this time.

Max slipped on the dressing robe and, after making sure no one was about to witness his state of undress, not to mention his cockstand, he headed for the study. Once inside, he found not her, not even a note, but a brandy that had been poured and set on the table next to a chair. He sat down, took up the brandy and shot half the liquid down his throat.

How much more of this was he expected to take? It seemed his rod was still anticipating some sort of reimbursement for being, for the last half-hour, in an uninterrupted state of stiffness, the way it poked through the opening of his robe.

Consuming the rest of his drink, Max set it back upon the table, when a sound came from behind the drapes.

Was it his imagination or had he actually heard something?

He stood, strode over to the window and yanked the drapes aside.

Katrina, his little mouse, stood there in nothing but her underpinnings.

Relieved, his gaze roamed over her and he noticed the tray from his silver tea service that should have been in the upstairs sitting room was lodged between her thighs. With a loud clang, it hit the floor at her feet.

Chapter Twenty-Three

Katrina dropped her gaze to Maxwell's stiff cock, which protruded from between the opening of his dressing robe. "I see I have your full attention now."

"Katrina, I—"

She poked her finger at his chest. "I didn't lure you up here to listen to you lecture me." She pushed harder and he backed up a step. "Sit down. I have a few things to say."

It took much less muscle than she'd imagined it would for him to concede. He sat in the chair next to the glass she'd previously filled with brandy. The snifter was empty now, so she retrieved the decanter and refilled it.

Barely looking at Maxwell, she handed him the glass and paced to the opposite side of the room.

"If there's one thing I despise, it's the lack of communication. I don't mean language barriers between different cultures, but flat-out, closed-mouthed failure to voice the exchange of ideas."

"When I—"

"Shut it!" She took a step toward him. Afraid she'd actually do him bodily harm if he attempted to obstruct her speech one more time, Katrina fisted her hands at her sides. "I'm not finished yet." She stomped her foot on the floor. "Occupy your mouth in some other way, Goddamn it. Drink!"

She watched him sink lower into his chair and raise the glass to his lips.

"Your sister has told me that when you get angry, you retreat—you stop talking and just...brood. But there is something you need to know—that sort of behavior is not going to work for me. When I get frustrated, it is imperative that I voice what's happening in my head or I will run mad. For weeks now, you have forbidden me to speak to you and honestly, I've had enough of it. I don't love Jimmy, I love you. I'm sorry you misinterpreted what you saw that day when I found out my friend wasn't dead, but what you thought you knew for certain is completely wrong. If you'd have heard me out that day, I wouldn't have been harboring this pain in my heart."

She paused, unsure whether she'd been getting through to him at all and, additionally, undecided as to whether she'd even allow him to speak if he tried. During her tirade, she'd watched the expression on his face go from blank, to something akin to interest, then back to blank again. It might be prudent at this juncture, she imagined, if she let him voice at least one of his thoughts. She crossed her arms over her chest in anticipation of...something.

"Question."

Well, that didn't take long. "Yes?"

"Did—? Did you say you love me?"

"You— I— Maxwell, is *that* what you unearthed out of everything I just told you?"

In one motion, he set his now empty glass down and stood. "Frankly, yes—at least... All right, to a great degree."

Now Katrina felt like sitting down. "Wha—?"

"Look. I understand. I shouldn't shut down when you need to talk. It comes down to this—when two people love each other they should communicate—and I agree entirely. That is why when I *retreat*, as you say, it's your job to regain my attention."

"L—love...each other?" She hoped with all her body and soul that this wasn't a gross misinterpretation.

He closed the distance between them. "Exactly." He put his arms around her waist, lifted her from the ground and held her tight against his chest. "I love you, too."

His admission melted away any other defense she may have possessed. "Oh, Maxwell," she said just before he kissed her. "How I've missed you."

"I'm sorry," he murmured between kisses. "I've been a fool."

She couldn't help but smile against his lips. "You won't hear any protestations on that account from me."

Maxwell chuckled. "You know, I kind of liked it when you took control the way you did."

She opened her eyes and found him gazing at her. "Really?"

His nod was nearly imperceptible.

"Should we, perhaps...explore this new-found...*submissive* fixation?"

"Yes." He kissed her again. "But not tonight. Tonight, I only want you—no toys, no playroom, no sex games—just you."

Undeniable joy bubbled up from the depths of her soul. She took hold of the collar of his robe and began to tug it off his shoulders.

"Wait. Not here. I want you in my bed."

"All right." She hadn't meant to whisper.

Maxwell loosened his grip and her feet came to rest on the floor. He took her by the hand and they made their way, as discreetly as possible, to his room.

Once inside she stood next to the bed and undid the front of her corset. It fell to the floor and she turned to see what he was doing. Facing her, he still clung to the bolt that he'd just slammed home and he leaned against the door, unmoving...his gaze on her body. She almost inquired as to what it was exactly that he was looking at when she realized it was she.

Katrina Harwood!

She'd have never thought she possessed such power over any man, but there he stood, mesmerized.

Slowly, Katrina turned her body away from him, but watched over her shoulder as his expression became very interested in her movements. Untying her drawers, she then hooked her thumbs beneath the waistband at her sides. She began nudging down first one side, then the other—the action painstakingly measured in tiny increments—her hips rocking, dipping down and up again with each movement. Lower and lower and lower the fabric slid along her skin. Aware that the top of her bum was about to be exposed, she paused and heard Maxwell's breathing from where she stood.

She turned to the side, showing Maxwell her profile, and continued the dance until she was sure her bottom was exposed. She pivoted to face him.

His gaze snapped from the white cotton fabric to her eyes. "Don't stop," he responded.

"I have something to show you, Maxwell," she whispered. "It's *very* naughty."

He swallowed, strode forward, stopped directly in front of her, then sank to his knees. "Show me."

"Are you sure you want to see it?"

"Mmm."

He lifted a hand, likely to assist, but she took a step backwards. "Ah, ah."

"Are you determined to kill me, Katrina?"

She chuckled. "Very well." She turned her back to him and let her drawers fall to her ankles. "Ready, then?"

"Katrina—" In his voice she detected a plea.

"Here it is." Pivoting on the ball of her foot, she faced him head on.

He licked his lips, staring at her pussy.

"Do you like it?" she asked, placing her hands on her hips. She'd sheared her pubic hairs so short that one could see every curve of the skin between her legs.

He nodded.

She slid her hands down toward where his gaze was fixated. "Do you want to touch it?"

He repeated the action.

With her fingers she delved into the folds. She peeled apart the skin and revealed her clitoris to him. "Do you want to taste it?"

In an instant, Maxwell was on his feet. The next thing she knew he'd tossed her onto the bed. With a moan he parted her knees and feasted on her pussy, murmuring adoration. His tongue wiggled her nubbin back and forth until just before she came, then he switched directions—up and down faster and faster. She opened her mouth, gulping in gusts of air until at last she balanced upon the crest of a great mountain.

He took this crucial moment to suckle her, and when he did, her orgasm hit like a fierce storm. She dug her fingers into his hair and pulled his head closer, pumping her hips, grinding against his mouth.

He moaned an enthusiastic sound and when the tremors subsided, she released him.

"That's my girl," he panted as if he'd been the one to climax. "I admire your zeal, my little mouse. But now it's my turn."

He climbed onto the bed and sank his cock into her. Katrina shrieked as the next orgasm assailed her. Her pussy throbbed in time to the spasms of her inner muscles.

"Fuck," he groaned and pumped into her harder. "You are so wet."

"Maxwell—" She wanted to convey the rapture she felt, but the only word that tumbled from her lips was his name—her love, the one who gave her such profound pleasure. She had no idea what she wanted of him—stop, go, faster, slower? Whatever the case, she had never imagined that these glorious physical sensations were capable of such breadth and width. Her body shuddered, climbing higher and higher.

Just when she thought she could stand no more, Maxwell increased his efforts once again. "I'm going to come, my sweet."

"Yes—" she panted. "Hurry. Before I shatter!"

He called to the heavens, shouting for God, echoing the very words Katrina was previously unable to perceive.

Finally, he shifted to lie next to her, his arm draped across her ribcage. She could have laid entwined with him in this manner forever.

"I love you, Maxwell."

"And I love you, Katrina."

* * * *

Martin opened the door to the newly restored carriage in front of the ship Jimmy had just booked passage on. He lowered the steps and Maxwell alighted, then handed Katrina down. They turned to watch Jimmy descend the two steps.

When Jimmy went to retrieve his two traveling valises from Martin, Katrina looked up at Maxwell for his approval and he nodded. She crooked a finger at him and he brought his face to hers.

"Thank you," she whispered and kissed his cheek.

Maxwell smiled, folded his arms across his chest, and leaned against the side of the carriage.

"Well, this is it," Jimmy said once he stood before Katrina, bags in hand.

Fighting a lump in her throat that had more to do with his bravery than his actual departure, Katrina set her hand in the crook of his elbow and together they started forward toward the gangplank.

Jimmy glanced over his shoulder at Maxwell and addressed Katrina quietly. "Shall I write?" He grinned.

"Very humorous. You realize all communications must cease between us if you are going to disappear."

They stopped at the base of the ramp and he turned to face Katrina. "I'll think of you every day."

"Jimmy. Don't. I want you to go and start a new life. How can you accomplish this if you dwell on…things that were never meant to be?"

"You've driven your point home, my sweet, but that doesn't mean I'll stop lovin' you."

Katrina placed a hand on his cheek. "I care about you so much, but you can't say things like that."

"But my heart says—"

"It's our hearts that get us into the most trouble." She let her palm slip from his face. "I think it's time you start listening to your head."

Jimmy sighed. "I know, I know."

The ship's horn blew so loudly that Katrina was tempted to cover her ears.

"God, I hope they don't do that while you're trying to sleep."

He chuckled. "Perhaps I'll appropriate it tonight and hide it in the brig."

"You'll do no such thing! No more stealing, now. I mean it," she said firmly. "This is a prime opportunity to start life anew. Not many people get a chance like this."

"Only you and I."

"We are the lucky ones, Jimmy."

He glanced up at the ship and rolled his shoulders back. "Onward then, I suppose."

Katrina reached up and gave him a peck on the cheek. "Be good."

He stepped up onto the wooden plank and looked back at her with that roguish smile of his. "Oh, I'm always that, love." Then he turned and up he went, disappearing through the portal.

At once Maxwell was next to Katrina. She swept a tear from her cheek and looked up at him.

"You'll miss him, I gather."

She shrugged. "As much as any dear friend, I would imagine."

"I know Simmons will."

"Simmons, how so?"

"According to him, your friend, Jimmy not only groomed the horses as if they were going to show, but he also weeded the herb and flower garden, polished every piece of silver in the house, and finished refurbishing my traveling coach that has sat dormant in my buggy port for a good two years."

"Um, did Simmons, by chance, *count* the silver when Jimmy was finished?"

Maxwell chuckled. "He did, indeed. He is very thorough."

"Yes, well, so is Jimmy," she murmured sardonically.

He put his arm about her waist and kissed the top of her head. "Not to worry. Simmons wouldn't have let Queen Victoria walk away with something that belonged to me."

They turned toward the carriage but took their time getting to it.

"I must say, Maxwell, for such a small space, your gardens are quite lovingly tended."

"Of course. What with Walters and Simmons belonging to Her Royal Majesty's garden club—"

Katrina pulled Maxwell to a stop. "Garden club? You told me they belonged to a gun club!"

"Oh, yes. I guess I did, didn't I?"

"Maxwell, you lied to me!"

"Lied? No... I merely mixed up my words."

"What?"

"Gun, garden... What is the difference? Not much, I'd imagine."

"You can't kill someone with a garden!"

"Are you aware, madam, of the adverse effects a good deal of hemlock in your tea will have on a body?"

"Maxwell..." Katrina tried so hard not to laugh, but to no avail.

He smiled. "There, see? No harm done." Placing a kiss on her forehead, he added, "I only minced my words to make you more at ease at the time."

Recovering, she wagged a finger at him. "Well, don't do it again. I want the truth from this moment on."

"Then I'm afraid you and I need to have a little talk," he said in a serious tone but pulled her into an embrace in contradiction of his words.

"What—? What's wrong?"

He sighed. "I'm afraid you can't come back with me to Hamilton Place."

Tiny pins pricked every nerve along her arms. "Wha—?"

"You can't come back to the house… Not unless you agree to become my wife."

Her breath left her, but only for a moment. "Oh, Maxwell!" She reached up and he lifted her higher, her toes dangling above the ground. Her tears began falling like a spring rain and she pressed her face against his shoulder.

"Is that a yes or a no?" she heard him ask.

She sniffed. "Yes, of course!"

He tightened his arms around her. "My beautiful mouse with the cat-like eyes."

Lifting her head she gazed at him. "I always thought they were oddly shaped.

"Not at all. In fact, your eyes are responsible for drawing me to you."

"And all this time I thought it was my bottom."

"Well, that too."

Katrina giggled at his smirk and he let her go.

They started for the carriage once again when he spoke, "So, where would you like to go on our honeymoon?"

"Heavens. What a question. How long do you suppose we'll be gone?"

"I don't know — a week, perhaps two."

She thought for a moment. "How about your playroom?" Katrina peered up at him. At his wicked grin, a searing thrill shot up her spine.

About the Author

Born and reared in Southern California, Genella deGrey longed to be your typical blonde, tanned, surfer girl but failed miserably. Unable to sit idle without falling asleep, she embarked upon several artistic endeavours. Make-up and set dressing for the entertainment industry, Resort Enhancement for The Walt Disney Company and writing sexy historical romance top the list of her favourite activities. A consummate closet goth and amateur music and (red) wine enthusiast, she is also a hopeless romantic awaiting the arrival of her very own Mr Romance/Soul Mate with whom to share the rest of her life.

Genella DeGrey loves to hear from readers. You can find her contact information, website details and author profile page at http://www.totallybound.com.

Totally Bound Publishing